Leslie is feeling lonely and depressed.

Granny laid a gentle arm across Leslie's shoulders. "Ye haven't been ta visit me yet, luv."

Leslie heard the unspoken message. Her dear Scottish friend wouldn't pry, but she wanted to listen if Leslie felt like talking. What would have sounded reproving from someone else, from Granny represented two opportunities. She could answer the obvious question with an explanation of her schedule. Or she could accept the offered comfort and open her heart. "I've been hoping Dylan would have time to come with me." Hearing her own words made her eyes fill with unstoppable tears. Once her heartache found a bit of release, a flood of emotion swamped her. The harder she tried to stop, the worse the storm became.

Granny pulled Leslie into her arms, absorbing the younger woman's tears into her shoulder. In her comforting embrace, the weeping gradually eased.

JANELLE BURNHAM is fast becoming one of **Heartsong Presents'** most popular authors in contemporary, as well as historical, romances. Janelle, who is single and lives in British Columbia, Canada, has been writing for over ten years.

Books by Janelle Burnham

HEARTSONG PRESENTS
HP53—Midnight Music
HP100—River of Peace
HP119—Beckoning Streams
HP139—Winding Highway

Dancing in
the Darkness

Janelle Burnham

Heartsong Presents

A note from the Author:
*I love to hear from my readers! You may write to me at
the following address:*   **Janelle Burnham**
                          Author Relations
                          P.O. Box 719
                          Uhrichsville, OH 44683

ISBN 1-55748-771-5

DANCING IN THE DARKNESS

Cover illustration by Kay Salem.

PRINTED IN THE U.S.A.

one

"Is Vince Carlson there?" The feminine voice sounded both cultured and apprehensive.

"Just a moment, please." Leslie set the phone down carefully, then ran up the stairs to tap on the door of what had become Vince's room after their younger brother's accident. Even after two months, she still thought of the room as Andrew's. "Vince, the phone's for you."

"Who is it?" he asked groggily.

"I don't know. I don't recognize her voice."

The door swung open abruptly. "*Her?*" He pushed past Leslie, a strange mixture of curiosity and satisfaction in his expression. However, his tone when he answered conveyed nothing but pleased charm. "This is Vince." His low, attentive murmur carried into the kitchen where Leslie spread cream cheese on crackers. How often since his adolescence had she heard just those tones in his phone conversations with one girl or another? From the time he'd been old enough to be aware of a gender different from his own, he'd had the knack of treating his current interest as if she were the only woman in the world. Even his multitude of former girlfriends still viewed him with unshaken admiration.

Leslie shook her head with private amazement and reached for a can of black olives with which to garnish the crackers. Her nephew, Li'l Brad, would be a year old tomorrow, and her own twenty-fourth birthday would be on Monday. In keeping with Carlson tradition, a family party had been planned for tomorrow afternoon. They would also celebrate the removal of Andrew's cast, which had encased his leg from toes to thigh since June.

A thump behind her announced his hobbling arrival. "Anything I can do to help?" He lowered himself into a chair beside the kitchen table and hoisted his long, newly released leg onto another chair in front of him.

Leslie glanced over her shoulder. His blond hair stood on end in typical disarray. He'd always been skinny, but illness had made him gaunt. Yet his eyes shone with alertness and a delight in living that hadn't been present since this nightmare had begun over eight months ago. Instinctively, she wanted to pamper him, but knew his teenaged pride wouldn't take it. "How about peeling potatoes?"

"Figured you'd give me drudge work," he grumbled playfully.

"I always could ask you to go mow the lawn."

The laugh she loved bubbled out. "Mom would probably kill us both if I even thought about it. According to her, I'm fragile enough to break if someone looks at me wrong."

Leslie silently admitted she felt the same. For most of his last semester in high school, his craving for alcoholic entertainment had turned him into a moody, obnoxious young person barely resembling the brother she'd practically raised. Just before graduation, an accident at the gravel pits involving a three wheeler and too much beer had almost claimed his life. Now he seemed to be on the mend both emotionally and physically, and she felt terrified something or someone would break the spell. "Are you suggesting since your cast is off, we can beat you up once or twice a day?" She plunked an empty bowl, a sack of potatoes, and a vegetable peeler in front of him.

He laughed again. "I dare you to try."

"It sounds like fun in here." Dad roamed into the large kitchen, peering over Leslie's shoulder, checking pots on the stove, and cuffing Andrew on the shoulder. "It's nice to see your leg again, son."

"You wouldn't be so sure of that if you could see under my pants." Andrew made a disgusted expression. "Two months without air and three liters of talcum powder have grossified my skin."

"Grossified?" Dad and Leslie asked in unison with accompanying grins. Andrew's unusual words had become a family joke, never failing to raise a reaction from whoever heard them.

"Yeah, turned it gross. You guys need a word building class."

"I think you do enough word building for us all." Dad snitched a cream cheese and black olive-laden cracker off the plate. "Mmm. Cracker things. I'd better get my share before Brad shows up tomorrow."

"Cream cheese hors d'oeuvres," Leslie corrected him. The first time she'd made the appetizer, her farmer brother-in-law had dubbed them "cracker things" before consuming most of them himself. The name had stuck, regardless of her attempts to impose a more cultured identification.

"Look who's joining the fun!" Dad exclaimed. "Howdy, hon'. You look like you had a good nap." He met his wife in the doorway with an embrace.

Leslie couldn't imagine one of her parents without the other. Though Mum was tall for a woman, Dad stood four inches taller. Gray streaked both his dark hair and her carefully styled reddish-brown curls. In fact, they both seemed much grayer than they had before the crisis had begun. She sighed to herself. Alcoholism had taken its toll on all of them. Yet Dad and Mum's love for each other had come through the struggle stronger than ever. Would she be able to love as successfully as her parents?

Memory of a pair of vivid green eyes brought a smile to her lips. Dylan Stoddard had become her friend, then her fiancé during the same six months that had threatened to consume her sanity. His gentle, solid support had helped her keep perspective even on the worst days. Though he'd been working for the last six weeks at a distant oil rig, thoughts of his steady love always brought delight.

The doorbell rang. Dad glanced at Leslie from where he stood, one arm around Mum's waist, looking over her shoulder as she began to make a salad. "You'd better get that, Leslie. I'm busy."

She chuckled and hurried to the entry. The figure just beyond the frosted glass looked familiar. She opened the door, then with a scream of delight, propelled herself into Dylan's waiting arms.

His laughter rumbled deep in his chest. "Missed me, did you?" He loosened his embrace only enough to tip her chin up and plant a long kiss on her lips. "I think I missed you, too."

Arms around each other's waists, the two stepped inside. Dad's mischievous face peered around the doorway of the kitchen. "Hello, son. Good to have you home."

Dylan hugged Leslie closer to him. "It's great to be home, Dr. C."

Leslie finally found her voice enough to ask, "What brings you to town?"

His eyes filled with delightful twinkles. "You and I have a dinner reservation at Papa Joe's in exactly one hour and forty-five minutes."

"Papa Joe's!" The unusual restaurant located in

Riverview, a small town about an hour's drive away, had been where Dylan had taken her on their first date. "That gives me forty-five minutes to get supper finished and my clothes changed."

All at once, Dad's tall form filled the kitchen doorway. "I don't think there's anything in here we can't cope with on our own."

"I'll keep track of them for you." Andrew's offer drifted from behind Dad.

Leslie knew when she'd been out-maneuvered. "In that case, I'll just go get beautiful."

"You already are," Dylan murmured, then gave her another quick kiss. "Hurry, though. I didn't drive six hours in from the boonies to visit with your dad."

Leslie laughed at her dad's pretended hurt expression and scampered up the stairs, already mentally sorting through her closet for an appropriate outfit. August heat still lingered, so she needed something light and cool. But by the time they finished their dinner, she'd probably need something to ward off the evening breeze. Her periwinkle blue short-sleeved jumpsuit would be perfect, she decided as she rinsed her hair under the shower. Thirty-minutes later, she bounded back down the stairs, a white summer blazer dangling off her arm.

Dylan wolf-whistled as his gaze took in her appearance, from the red-glinted curls fluffed around her shoulders to her white low-heeled pumps. "You never cease to amaze me, Les. I've seen women take twice as long to get ready as you did, and they never look half as beautiful."

A teenaged groan erupted from the kitchen. "Let's get out of here," Leslie suggested before Andrew's teasing could get embarrassing.

The drive to Riverview seemed to pass in moments. She

snuggled as close to Dylan as the middle console would allow, reveling in his company. He glanced her way occasionally with the gentle smile meant only for her. Once they arrived, the waiter directed them to a secluded table on the patio. They ordered from the tabloid-sized menus which, along with plush parrots dangling from the mirrored ceiling, were part of Papa Joe's unique atmosphere. She couldn't help grinning, still amazed that this dark-haired, distinguished looking man wanted to marry her. His long-sleeved white shirt, forest green tie, and black dress pants set off his muscular figure perfectly.

His eyes glowed with affection. "That beautiful smile tells me you're thinking something I'd like to know about." He covered her hand with one of his calloused, tanned ones.

Until he'd come into her life, Leslie had been unable to associate the word beautiful with herself. At five foot eight, she felt neither gracefully tall nor attractively petite, just nondescript. She had always avoided analyzing her features, aware that she'd inherited the large Carlson nose and a mouth too wide to be called pretty. Yet Dylan's admiration made her feel gorgeous. "I can't believe you're here. I was thinking about you, and there you were."

Their waiter's arrival interrupted conversation. Dylan ordered the steak special, and Leslie her favorite meal at Papa Joe's, barbecued chicken. When he withdrew, Dylan winked. "Your dad knew I was coming. I called him a couple of days ago to make sure I wouldn't be stealing you away from one of those famous Carlson family parties."

"So that's why he was so busy when you rang the doorbell. What did he say?" Initially attracted to Dylan because of his friendship with her dad, Leslie always wondered about their conversations concerning her.

"He said it was high time you had a birthday dinner you

didn't have to cook."

She felt the familiar urge to defend her family, until gentle pressure on her hand reminded her she didn't need to make explanations to this man.

"I wasn't criticizing, sweetheart." His eyes softened with loving intensity.

She intertwined her fingers with his. "I should know that by now. I just hate the insinuation I'm hard done by." She leaned away from the table so their waiter could place her food in front of her.

"And that's why your dad and I check up on you. You refuse to complain even when things get too much. How's my future mother-in-law doing?"

Leslie grinned at the reference to their marriage a year from now. "Amazingly well. She's spent most of her time with Andrew since he was hurt. I thought his accident would send her back into depression, but it seems to have had the opposite effect."

"Meanwhile, you're once again doing all the cooking, cleaning, shopping, and laundry because you don't want to take her away from him."

She let his loving gaze reassure her as she nodded.

"How is that going to change once classes start again?"

"I guess that depends on Andrew."

He shook his head. "No, my love, it depends on you. By the end of August, he should no longer need round-the-clock attention. You might even be doing both him and your mum a favor by giving her something else to claim her attention."

Leslie smiled, remembering a scene earlier in the day. "You could be right. Just this morning he decided he didn't want to be helped in the shower since Dad wasn't home to do it. Mum hovered outside the bathroom door the entire time, asking him every thirty seconds if he was all right. She was sure he'd lose his balance since he's still so weak."

"What's next for him now that his cast is off?"

"Several visits to a specialist in Bayfield, about four months of intensive physiotherapy, and rest."

"I'd imagine." Dylan signaled for a refill of their water glasses. "Spleens aren't meant to take the kind of beating his did, and it will be awhile before his leg is ready to function normally. How is he doing otherwise?"

Leslie hesitated. "I wish I knew for sure. Being bedridden, he hasn't had an opportunity to either refuse or accept a drink. He won't admit he wouldn't have been riding the three-wheeler at the gravel pits if he hadn't been drunk."

"How is Vince handling that bit of denial?" He grinned understandingly.

She smiled, too. Her older brother's intolerance of Andrew's "unchristian behavior" had been a chief source of family tension before the accident. "He's been working long shifts at the sawmill, so he's not home much. My guess is that he thinks Andrew's brush with death has cured him."

"And Karen?"

"She and Brad aren't around often enough to make a difference. Summertime is always hectic out at the farm, so she has enough to do keeping track of her husband and baby." She savored the last spicy bite of chicken.

"Relief is felt by all," he quipped, smiling at the waiter who appeared as if on cue to clear away their empty plates.

Leslie laughed. Only with Dylan could she share the frustration of her older sister's well-meaning but useless advice. "She can be a pain, can't she?"

"I'm just glad she's going to be my sister-in-law and not my mother-in-law."

"You've done a lot of thinking about these relationships,"

she teased.

"Of course. I have to know what I'm getting into."

Before Leslie could reply, waiters and waitresses surrounded their table. On cue, they struck up an off-key version of "Happy Birthday" that attracted the attention of other diners. A waiter placed a massive piece of cheesecake bearing a sparkler before her. Dylan's obvious delight eliminated the embarrassment she would have felt had anyone else planned this kind of surprise. When the song ended, someone handed her a small, wrapped package. "We were asked to present this to you, ma'am, and told we could watch you open it."

Checking Dylan's face for reassurance, she saw barely suppressed excitement with a hint of apprehension. She peeled back the wrapping and peered into the box, only to find a smaller wrapped package within. Removal of three more layers revealed a small, velvet jewelry box. "Is this what I think it is?"

Dylan just grinned. "Open it and find out."

She flipped back the lid to reveal a diamond ring. The large center diamond sat in a random setting of smaller diamonds interspersed with tiny emeralds. "Oh, Dylan!"

"Hey, it's an engagement ring!" one of the waiters announced, and everyone, other diners included, clapped and whistled.

Dylan leaned forward so she could hear him above the applause. "It's not a typical engagement ring, but I thought you might like it anyway."

"It's gorgeous, and far fancier than anything I'd dreamed of. I hope it wasn't too expensive." She only vaguely noticed the crowd around their table dispersing.

"There is no such thing as too expensive when it's for you."

"Thank you." She leaned across the table to brush his lips with a quick kiss. "Would you put it on my finger for me?"

"With pleasure, milady." He held the ring poised over her hand. "This is your last chance, Miss Leslie Carlson. Are you sure you want to marry me next summer?"

Though he spoke playfully, she felt the current of emotion. "I'd marry you tomorrow if I could."

His gaze never left her face while he fitted the cool metal over the third finger of her left hand. "This tells the whole world I'm the most blessed man alive. Now comes the hard part—waiting."

She wrapped her newly adorned hand around his. "Like I said, if you weren't so determined I finish my last year of Bible school, I'd marry you tomorrow. I just wish we didn't have to be separated so much. Have any churches contacted you yet?"

"That's something else I wanted to discuss with you. I've had just one offer, and it's pretty unusual." He seemed to be looking for something deep inside her.

"Where is it?"

"Nipson."

Her eyes widened in surprised. "What church?"

"Heritage Christian Assembly."

Her home church. If he accepted the offer, he'd be around all year. "I didn't know Pastor Quillan was leaving."

Dylan shook his head. "He's not. That's what's so unusual. He and the board feel he needs an assistant, but they can't afford to pay me for it. I'd have to find a different job since roughnecking isn't exactly suited to weekly appearances at church. Basically, I'd be working two full-time jobs, which wouldn't leave much time for us."

"Which could be an advantage for me in my studies."

She grinned teasingly.

He acknowledged the joke with a squeeze of her hand. "Wise guy. I'm still not sure I want to accept."

"Why not?" She hadn't seen this side of his personality before. Usually he knew exactly what he felt was right to do and simply did it.

"It's going to be hard in many ways."

"I've never known you to avoid something simply because it was difficult."

"But this decision could make things difficult for you."

The unexpected response left her speechless for a moment. "Why?"

"Because Heritage is your church home, and because since everyone there will soon know of our engagement, you're going to get the same kind of pressure you'd get if you were already my wife." A broad smile stretched his face on the last two words. "You have enough to handle at home without my adding to the burden. I don't want anything to hamper your finishing this last year. If stress causes you to fail a course, I have to wait another semester to marry you."

Leslie heard the intense concern behind his teasing words. "Dylan, have you asked our Heavenly Father what He wants you to do?"

He nodded. "I can't think of any man I'd rather work under than Pastor Quillan. The next ten years wouldn't be long enough for me to absorb all the wisdom he's accumulated."

"Then it's up to our Lord to shield me from any unnecessary stress. My dad was on the board of deacons for most of my growing up years. I know a bit about what to expect."

Moisture glinted in his eyes and he swallowed several

times before he spoke in an emotion-roughened voice. "After all you've been through in the last six months, you're telling me you're ready to take on another challenge. You're amazing. We'd better get out of here so I don't embarrass you by kissing you in front of all these people."

two

Sighing to herself, Leslie switched off the vacuum cleaner. Since six this morning, she'd been busy with housecleaning. Not that this made today any different from other Saturdays, but she'd been tensely listening all day for the sound of the family car pulling into the driveway. Mum, Dad, and Andrew had left for Bayfield day before yesterday for Andrew's appointment with an internal specialist. Their local physician, Dr. Farr, had been pleased with the way Andrew's leg had healed, but wanted an internalist to examine the damaged spleen. "The spleen is one of the more mysterious parts of the body," he'd explained. "When it works properly, we don't think much about it. But when it doesn't, it can be fatal. I'd feel a lot better having Dr. Wallace's analysis." The appointment had been yesterday, and the family was due home today. Logic told her they wouldn't return until early evening. Still, she'd feel uneasy until they arrived.

The ringing telephone startled her so badly she dropped the vacuum power head. *That's the result of getting yourself so worked up, stupid*, she chided herself, hurrying to answer. "Hello?"

"A marvelous afternoon to you, gorgeous!" a welcome voice laughingly replied, followed by a slight echo.

"Dylan! You sound like you're talking from the bottom of a barrel." She settled herself on the floor below the wall-mounted phone with what felt like an utterly ridiculous grin.

17

"I'm calling from the radio phone out here at work. I've almost made up my mind about the church and wanted you to be in on it."

"Almost? I've never known you to be almost about any decision." She tried to keep her tone light.

"All my decisions up until now have only involved me." Seriousness permeated his words. "You're part of my future now as well as my heart, and I want to make sure I do what's best for both of us. Have you been praying about Pastor Quillan's offer?"

"Sort of. I've mostly just been asking God to show you what to do." She wished she could reach across the miles and hold his hand.

"I appreciate that, honey, but this will affect your world, too. How do you feel about it now that you've had time to consider?"

Whatever he felt was right would please her the most, but she knew that wasn't the answer he wanted to hear. "I'm not afraid of the possibilities, Dylan. Heritage has been a wonderful church family in which to grow up. If this is where you feel you should be, I'm happy to be here, too."

"Are you sure?" Earnest apprehension now filled his voice.

Deliberately, she lowered her voice almost to a whisper in order to get his attention. "Sweetheart, there will be potential struggles wherever you go. If you work with Pastor Quillan, at least we'll be in the same town. We'll be in it together."

He chuckled softly but not convincingly. "That's what scares me and gives me courage, too. Don't I sound like pastor material?"

"You sound like an incredibly caring man who wants

with all his heart to do what God wants him to do. I'm one blessed lady to have you for a future husband."

"Future only for a year," he reminded teasingly, then paused. "Les, I'm going to do it."

"Are you sure?" she mimicked.

Another long pause, then the confidence she'd grown to love came soaring through the wires. "Positive. Somehow talking with you has helped me dispose of the confusion. I'd chat with you longer, but I promised Pastor Quillan I'd give him my answer by three o'clock."

She checked her watch. "You have precisely two minutes to dial. Think you can manage it?"

"I'd do better if you were here. I love you and miss you terribly."

"I miss you, too."

"Don't you love me?" His tone now filled with pretend hurt.

"Of course I do, you goof. You now only have one minute before your deadline."

He chuckled. "I just don't want to hang up. Bye, sweetheart." The line went dead abruptly.

Leslie hung up the phone with a smile. She loved Dylan's crazy sense of humor that made a joke out of almost anything without ever hurting another person's feelings. Something inside her had settled into calmness now that his plans for the next year had been settled. She wished he and Dad hadn't insisted she finish her last year of Bible school. She'd much rather have spent today doing housekeeping for herself and her husband. Instead, she'd cleaned up after Vince's early morning breakfast, put through five loads of laundry, cleaned both bathrooms from floor to ceiling, and waxed every linoleum floor in the house. The abandoned vacuum reminded her of the other job she'd finished. She needed something to keep herself busy until her family arrived.

The phone rang again. She finished returning the vacuum to the closet before she answered. "Hello?"

Karen's agitated voice replied. "Are they home yet?"

"Not yet." Leslie worked to keep irritation out of her tone. Her older sister never failed to turn the simplest situations into crises. "They usually don't make it back until well after six."

"I know, but with it getting dark earlier in the evening I thought Dad might make sure they left Bayfield earlier."

"Which would mean they'd drive in the dark in the morning instead of in the evening. Besides, it doesn't get dark until after seven."

"At least in the morning, Dad would be fresh and alert. I'm surprised they haven't called."

Leslie shook her head in exasperation. She should have known better than to try to use logic to calm Karen. When Karen decided to get excited about something, only her husband Brad could talk sense into her. Even he wasn't always successful. "They usually don't call. Would you like me to have them phone you when they get in?"

"I'm just worried, Leslie. If I just knew they were okay, I'd feel better." A hint of panic crept into Karen's voice.

"Karen, until we hear otherwise, we have to assume they're fine." A wail in the background provided a different topic. "Let me guess. Li'l Brad just tried to climb up the chair and pulled it over on himself."

The diversion worked. Karen giggled. "Actually he was climbing up the bookcase and his dad pulled him off. He's not nearly as hurt as he sounds."

"So does Brad have all the hay off?"

"Yes. We had a great crop this year. We have enough for

our stock and about 300 bales we can sell. Come spring, we'll probably be able to buy our own registered bull."

Leslie had a hard time feeling excited about the farm news, but at least her sister was no longer having hysterics. "How did the garden do this year?"

"We have about 100 pounds of potatoes, and enough canned vegetables to carry us through the winter. Brad will slaughter a pig and a steer next week, which will fill our freezer, and we've already frozen a dozen chickens. Once Brad gets the woodpile stocked up, we'll be set for winter. Anyway, I've got to go and feed my men. Talk to you later."

Leslie chuckled to herself. Karen's moods were like the wind, shifting at will. All a person had to do was find a topic of conversation that related to the farm or either of the Brads. She glanced into the kitchen where a loaf of French bread sat thawing on the counter. The travelers wouldn't want a big supper, so meal preparation could wait until they arrived. In a matter of minutes, she could have the loaf filled with cut meat, sliced cheese, tomatoes, lettuce, and pickles.

She trudged upstairs to her room. Maybe cleaning out her small filing cabinet of Bible school notes and projects would keep her occupied. She wanted to get the job done before classes started in just over a week, anyway. Stoutly resisting the temptation to browse through a file labeled "Dylan," she emptied the top drawer onto her floor. She'd miss finding notes from her sweetheart in unexpected places. At least once a day last semester, she'd encountered a cartoon drawing, a verse of Scripture, a joke, or a simple love note tucked into her bag, textbook, boot, or jacket. His creativity had been limitless, and she'd saved every scrap. However, this afternoon's objective was organization, not sentimental reminiscing. Some class notes, like English 302, could be trashed. Others, like those from Dr. Jonas's lectures on the book of Isaiah, she wanted to save. After a couple of hours, she'd cleared the top drawer for this year's files and condensed her previous three years of Bible school notes into the other drawer.

The paper-filled garbage bag strained under the weight as she lugged it down the stairs and outside to the garbage stand. Returning to the empty house, she flopped on a chair in the living room, then changed her mind and went outside to the porch swing. The air still felt like summer. A few wispy clouds drifted across the pale blue sky. She tipped her head against the padded backrest, closed her eyes, and breathed deeply. There were still half a dozen projects she wanted to complete before school resumed in ten days, but it felt heavenly to do nothing for a little while. Her mind drifted to its favorite thought pattern. What was Dylan doing now? If he were in town, they'd probably be going for a walk together or taking a drive in the countryside. He hadn't said when he'd be moving back to Nipson. She grinned. After mentally preparing herself all summer for a long separation, she could hardly believe he'd actually be here all winter. *Don't get too excited*, she reminded herself. *With two jobs, he's probably going to be so busy, you won't see much of him.* But the little bits of time they'd snatch together would still be more than if he were working in some distant town. In less than a year, they'd probably be married and in a home of their own. With her foot braced on the porch floor, she moved the swing back and forth in a gentle rocking motion and let her imagination explore the exciting possibilities. She didn't realize she'd fallen asleep until the sound of a slammed car door jolted her awake.

Dad followed Mum up the walkway toward her. "You look like you were having some pleasant dreams."

"Yeah." Leslie stumbled to her feet, still feeling disoriented from her unplanned nap. The back of her neck hurt from the awkward angle at which she'd leaned on the swing. "I didn't expect you home so soon."

"It is almost six," Andrew informed her disdainfully, then grinned. "Guess what? The doctor says I should be feeling one hundred percent by the time basketball season starts."

Her sleepiness vanished in an instant. She locked her younger brother in a neck-crushing hug. "That's fantastic, Andrew! You can tell me all about while I get supper ready." She hurried to the kitchen to slice tomatoes.

Andrew hoisted himself onto the counter and crunched on the pickle he'd snitched. "Monday we'll double my physio from an hour a day. When school starts, they'll reschedule me for late afternoon so I can still get two hours every day, then build up to three after a month or so. Dr. Wallace says as long as I still feel good and Dr. Farr keeps an eye on me, I can work as hard as I want to get in shape for the team." The thump of the front door announced Vince's arrival from work. Andrew slid off the counter. "I'll tell ya the rest later," he mumbled. Moments later, his bedroom door clicked shut.

Leslie felt a familiar twist in her stomach. It hurt to have the two brothers she loved so dearly at odds with one another. The quarrel had begun in the spring when Vince had attempted to lecture Andrew about his drinking. Andrew, in turn, had pointed out some unpleasant truths about Vince's character. Until Andrew's accident, the two could rarely be in the same room without a war of words erupting. Then during that interminable night when only a doctor's skill and God's goodness stood between Andrew and death, Vince's attitude had seemed to soften. Andrew's continuing discomfort in his brother's presence, however, indicated Vince had neither asked forgiveness from Andrew nor granted it to him. She cut the now stuffed French loaf into individual portions while fervently wishing he could swallow his insufferable pride and begin winning Andrew's confidence again.

According to Carlson tradition, both brothers joined the family for supper. Only on rare occasions—other than illness—had any of them been allowed to miss participating in the evening meal. As always, supper conversation remained amiable. Dad had long ago established this time of the day as a "no conflict zone." Arguments might resume later in the evening, but during the meal everyone was expected to be polite if not friendly. Tonight, the five of them lingered around the table after the sandwiches had disappeared. Though neither brother spoke to the other, both participated in the general chatter. Finally Dad pushed his chair back. "This has been a nice homecoming. Thanks for supper, Leslie." Something in his eyes diluted her discouragement, yet showed her a burden he wanted to share.

Evening sunshine streamed through the kitchen window as she stacked dishes beside the sink. She'd have liked nothing better at the moment than to return to the porch swing and enjoy what she knew would be one of summer's last evenings. In no time, the air would become crisp with a fall chill. But supper dishes needed to be washed and the kitchen cleaned up before she took any personal time. Memories of last spring brought a sigh. Before Andrew's accident, the household had settled into an easy division of chores that left her with an unprecedented amount of time for herself. It hadn't been easy at first, after being solely responsible since grade six. However, at Dad's insistence, she'd become accustomed to sharing the load.

Then Andrew had been injured. When he'd finally come home from the hospital, it had seemed natural for Leslie to once again assume the entire housekeeping load so Mum could preserve her limited energy for him. Dad had helped when he could, but he'd often been needed in Andrew's room. Leslie hadn't expected any extra help from Vince. He'd moved back home from Brad and Karen's right after the accident. Within a couple of days, he'd been hired at the mill. He had never been good at helping around the house, and shift work made him even worse.

The subject of her thoughts grabbed a dish towel and reached for dishes she'd just lifted from the steaming rinse water. She smiled to herself. How like him. Just when she thought he didn't see anything beyond his own interests, he surprised her. She directed a grin at his face—so much like her own, though his features gave him the rugged good looks so many girls found irresistible. "To what do I owe this honor?"

Easy charm glowed through his smile. "It's been awhile since we've had a chat. I've learned the only way I get a chance to visit with you is if I help with whatever you're doing."

"Whatever the reason, I appreciate it."

"Quite a sparkler you've got there." He nodded toward her engagement ring lying on the windowsill.

She always removed it while cooking or doing dishes for fear of damaging its luster. "Isn't it pretty? Dylan picked it out himself."

"You really love him." The statement held a hint of a question. His tone reminded her of many of the conversations they'd had while growing up. Vince had always been her protector. Any boy who showed interest in her had to win Vince's approval. As it had turned out, even those who passed his inspection didn't meet her standards. Until Dylan, she hadn't met anyone with the elusive qualities for which she'd been looking. Even so, Vince had treated Dylan with barely concealed hostility until this summer.

A lump of emotion blocked her throat. Unable to speak, she simply met his inquiring gaze and nodded.

"He's a lucky man to be loved by you."

The unexpected compliment almost caused her to drop the dish she'd been washing. Her older brother expressed affection easily, sometimes flippantly. But this statement made her feel like he viewed her as a special woman, not simply his kid sister. She looked into his eyes again. "Thanks, Vinny."

Unfamiliar red tinged his jawline. "Just thought you should know." He vanished from the kitchen as suddenly as he'd appeared.

She picked up his abandoned dish towel and finished his job. Two mugs of water heated in the microwave oven while she wiped drips from the counter, rinsed out the sinks and hung the dish cloth over the oven door handle. The sparkle of her ring on the windowsill caught her attention. She slowly slid the ring onto her finger, admiring the extravagant setting. Every time she saw it, she felt thrilled to her toes with Dylan's immense love. If she closed her eyes, she could feel again the long hug he'd given her before leaving Sunday evening. Stirring mocha mix into one mug and chocolate in the other, she carried both steaming drinks into Dad's study.

As she expected, his Bible lay open on his desk. He looked up from his reading of the Psalms to accept the cup of mocha. "Thanks, daughter. I thought you might be joining me." His eyes looked tired.

"Where's Mum?" She settled into an armchair close to his desk.

Just the mention of his wife brightened his gaze. "Enjoying a leisurely bubble bath."

Leslie chuckled. "I'll never be able to understand what she finds so luxurious about sitting in soapy water."

Dad's grin teased her gently. "Sitting never has been your favorite activity." He sipped his hot beverage.

She did the same, letting the comforting silence ease her tension. A door slammed, Vince's heavy tread came down the stairs, then the front door closed with a bang. She looked up to see Dad watching her. "So how was the trip?"

Dad shrugged. "Pleasantly uneventful. Both Mum and Andrew slept most of the way there and back."

"He seems pretty happy over the doctor's prognosis."

"Physiologically, Andrew is doing better than Dr. Wallace expected. He's even written his consent for Andrew to begin intensive physiotherapy next week along with some supervised exercise to start getting him in shape for the basketball season."

She sensed something unspoken in his reply. "Do you mean he anticipates no long term effects from the accident?"

Sadness stretched itself across Dad's expression. "Not precisely. He is concerned about how Andrew's body may respond to alcohol in the future, and recommends Andrew avoid it completely."

"How did Andrew respond to that?"

"He desperately wants all of us, including himself, to think it won't be a problem."

"Do you think it will be?" She suppressed a sudden shiver.

Dad's gaze held hers firmly. "Addictions don't vanish overnight, Les. His accident scared him thoroughly, but we have no way of knowing if he'll stay scared after he's back on his feet with the old crowd."

No response came readily to mind. She realized how intensely she'd hoped her brother's brush with death had cured his alcoholism.

"Leslie." Dad's quiet voice compelled her to look at him again. "Worry isn't going to help Andrew. He has to make his own decisions and live with their consequences. Besides, there's another young man who will benefit far more from your concern than Andrew will."

She felt her expression soften at the allusion. "He called today."

"And?" Dad's eyebrows raised questioningly.

"He's been trying to make up his mind about a job offer from Pastor Quillan." Excitement brought a smile to her face as she outlined the details.

An answering smile brightened Dad's expression. "Has he decided yet?"

She nodded. "Despite his worries about how it will affect me, he was going to call Pastor Quillan this afternoon and accept."

"How do you feel about it?" He leaned back in his chair and lifted his legs onto the corner of his desk as if settling in for a long conversation.

"I think it's a terrific opportunity for him. Like I told him, you were on the board of deacons for most of my growing up years, so I'm not unprepared for spotlight. Besides, I'd might as well get used to it now. It will only get worse when he is called to a church of his own." She set her empty mug on the floor beside her chair.

He folded his hands across his stomach, which was only slightly rounded despite his age. "It could be harder than you think, daughter. Church people are more possessive and critical of their pastoral families than of families in other leadership positions. Since you've grown up in this church, a lot of people will still view you as a child in need of guidance. The two of you will probably get more advice than you dreamed possible."

"Advice about what?"

He chuckled. "Absolutely everything. Even areas of your life you thought were nobody's business but your own. Your wedding date, the amount of time you spend together, the amount of time you can't spend together, whether you should hold hands in public, the kind of clothes you should wear. A number of people will tell you their opinions hoping you'll pass the word along to Dylan and the pastor. Others you thought were good friends won't talk as much with you because you're a de facto part of the pastoral staff." He laughed again softly. "We have a great congregation at Heritage Christian Assembly, but we're all still human. I'm glad your fiancé has some reservations before committing you to that kind of life."

"I've never seen him so unsure of himself," Leslie admitted. "I tried to reassure him, but I don't know if I helped."

"I'm sure your support means a lot to him. Speaking from experience, though, it's scary making a decision which will have a significant affect on the life of someone you love."

"He's more concerned about me than he is about himself. I'd often wondered what it would be like to be loved like this, and now it's happened, it feels too good to be true."

Dad dropped his feet to the floor so he could lean forward. "Don't give that thought room to grow, Leslie," he said with intensity. "Dylan's offering you the kind of love Scripture says a man should show his wife, but he will continue to do so only if you accept it. Mutual giving and receiving are what will keep your relationship strong. If you start doubting him now, you won't have the strength he needs when times get tough."

three

Throughout the following week, Leslie found herself watching Andrew for clues. He seemed to prefer his own company to being with his family, but didn't display the sullen withdrawal he had earlier in the year. He also appeared to avoid Vince as much as possible, for which Leslie couldn't blame him. Vince's attitude toward him barely lingered within the limits of civility.

But, she reminded herself Saturday afternoon, if there had been one lesson she'd learned in the last year, it had been not to make her family's problems her own. She opened the half-finished novel on her headboard. Not only would it be good escape, but she probably wouldn't get another opportunity to finish it once school resumed on Monday. Gradually, the fictitious world of a Christian international antique dealer closed in around her.

Four chapters later, a knock on her door pulled her back to reality. The door opened a bit and Dad's face peered through. "I just talked to your favorite fiancé," he said with a grin. "He said to tell you he'll be by in an hour to take you for supper."

"Thanks, Dad." Giddy anticipation replaced the lingering tendrils of worry. "I haven't started anything for supper so you guys will have to fend for yourselves."

"Actually, Mum and I are going on a date of our own. I'm sure between the two of them, Andrew and Vince can come up with something."

"If they don't kill each other first." She grinned wryly to

cover the cynical words.

Dad's eyebrows lifted in amused understanding, but he shut the door without reply.

She hurried through a shower, pausing for only a couple of moments to admire her sparkling emerald through the spray. From the back of her closet she pulled her favorite outfit, a mint-green dress with elbow-length sleeves and a long, swishy skirt. The last time she'd worn it had been in the spring for another spur-of-the-moment dinner with Dylan. She left her hair loose around her face the way he liked it, then fluffed and sprayed the curls around her ears to make her rhinestone earrings more visible. Cream pantyhose and high-heeled sandals completed her attire with only five minutes to spare. She perched in her window seat to watch for the familiar yellow jalopy he referred to as "the Princess." When she saw it coming up the street, she hurried downstairs and outside.

Dylan met her halfway up the walk with a bear hug and a wraparound grin. "I'm home, sweetheart." He looked breathtakingly handsome in gray dress pants and shirt with a green tie almost the exact shade of his eyes.

She leaned back to put a hand on either side of his face and pull his head down for a long, sweet kiss. "And I'm glad. Where are we going for dinner?"

The mischievous twinkles she loved lit his eyes. "You'll just have to wait and see." With an arm around her shoulders, he guided her to the car and opened the passenger door. "Your chariot awaits, my lady."

While he walked around to his side of the car, Leslie tilted her head back against the seat and closed her eyes. This battered vehicle felt like a refuge. The light scent of Dylan's cologne lingered. She felt the other end of the bench seat give under his weight as he maneuvered his length under the steering wheel. His kiss touched her lips before she was aware he'd leaned toward her. She opened her eyes to look directly into his, while his thumb rubbed gently across her cheekbone. "You look like you need a nap more than dinner," he offered.

"That's where you're wrong, Pastor Stoddard." She lifted her hand to pull his away from her face and into her lap. "I'm just relaxed, not tired."

"Then where did you get those smudges under your eyes?" His green ones communicated affectionate concern.

She hoped her smile and teasing tone would let him know she wasn't trying to hide anything, but neither did she feel like starting their date with a discussion about her family. "Stress, most likely from not having you around."

His smile told her he understood. "Then it sounds like a date is exactly what you need." He straightened in his seat and started the car. After backing out of the driveway, he turned the car away from the downtown area.

She watched his strong, calloused hands on the steering wheel. "I didn't know supper came with a scenic tour of Nipson."

"And I didn't know location was as important on a date as the right company," he teased back, reaching over for her hand.

"As usual, you're right." Contentment seeped into her bones.

He glanced her way with a grin. "You look like you're practically purring."

"I wish there were a way to capture emotional moments the way we can remember events with photographs. This is one I'd like to frame and hang where I could look at it all the time."

"It means a lot to me to hear you say so." He squeezed

her hand.

"What do you mean?"

"One of the things I love most about you is your depth of emotion. Many people are so shallow, they only feel the big things in life. You, on the other hand, respond emotionally to everything around you, but you've worked hard at making yourself appear as unaffected as you think you ought to be. When you go to the effort of putting your feelings into words, it tells me you trust me enough to be yourself." He stopped the car in front of an average-looking apartment building and unbuckled his seat belt. "Here we are. Ready to come look at something?"

Leslie just stared at him mutely, still clinging to his hand in her lap. In four sentences, he had described her heart. His intimate understanding made her feel cherished. How could she respond to something so precious?

A tender smile slowly spread into his eyes and across his face. "You look a little shell-shocked." He gathered her into a hug. "I didn't say what I did to make you feel like you had to live up to anything. You're the love of my life just exactly the way you are."

"Thanks, Dylan," she whispered against his broad chest. He held her close for a few more minutes, then she pulled away. "You wanted to show me something?"

He hurried around to open her door, looking like a small boy in his anticipation. "Right this way, m'lady." He fitted a key into the lock on the double glass doors and held one open for her. Gray carpet with flecks of green, blue, and pink lined the hallway in front of them. Once again clasping her hand, he led her up two flights of stairs and down another hallway before stopping in front of a door labeled "316," which he unlocked and motioned her through.

A small but bright kitchen opened off to her left with a

little table at the opposite end. To her right, a wide closet covered the wall up to a doorway into a tiny bathroom. Just beyond it, a wall formed a short hallway between the kitchen and the rest of the apartment. She followed around the corner to the open living area. The part closest to the kitchen contained a couch and some bookshelves. A bed had been pushed into the far corner, giving an illusion of a separate room. A patio door beside the couch led to a tiny balcony. She could see the Heritage Christian Assembly building just a couple of blocks away.

Dylan had taken a route through the kitchen and now met her in the doorway between kitchen and living area. "What do you think?"

She put her arms around his waist. "If it's yours, I like it."

"It's mine, though only for a year. I'll have to upgrade next summer."

His words evoked the picture that was never far from her imagination. Though she always imagined them living in a house, an apartment would be just as good. As long as it was their home together. Being held in his hug made the waiting both easier and more difficult.

"As you can tell, I'm going to need some help with interior decorating." He gestured with one arm toward the bare mattress on the bed and the bare window frames before tightening his embrace.

"When did you find it?"

"I just signed the lease this afternoon. Pastor and Mrs. Quillan loaned me the couch and bookshelves, and I asked my parents last week to send the bed up on the bus."

"Do you have any bedding at all?"

"Nope." He looked blissfully unconcerned, gazing affectionately into her face rather than at their surroundings.

"What about dishes?"

"What for?" he teased, planting a kiss on her mouth.

Though it had been only a few weeks since they'd seen each other last, it seemed like forever. Their kiss lengthened, filled with the love mere letters and phone calls couldn't communicate. Familiar emotions, made unfamiliar by growing ardor, created a wave of feeling that carried them both on its delightful swell. Then simultaneously, they became aware of their surroundings and pulled apart, shaken and dazed.

"This probably wasn't my brightest idea," he whispered.

She nodded in agreement, not trusting her voice to remain steady. The strength of what had flowed between them both excited and frightened her.

Wordlessly, not touching each other, they moved out of the suddenly too-private apartment. The lock snapped into place with a loud click, breaking the intensity of the moment. When they'd settled into the car, he didn't turn the ignition key immediately. She couldn't interpret the expression in his eyes when he looked at her. He turned on the seat so his back leaned against the door and curled one leg on the seat between them.

"Les, I'm scared." The rough whisper bore no resemblance to his usual jubilant tone.

Though as shaken as he, she sensed more behind his reaction than the passion that had developed so unexpectedly. She waited for him to continue.

"We almost stumbled into something we wouldn't have been able to control." He seemed to be thinking out loud. "Maybe I should apologize to you, but I don't know what I'd be apologizing for. I love you, Leslie, and I want to make you as much a part of the details of my life as possible. I took you up there only because I wanted to show you where I'll be living until we're married. That kiss was only meant to tell you how much I'm looking forward to the day we move into our own home together." A short, harsh laugh erupted from him. "I guess I told you, all right."

For the first time since she met him, she felt like the steadier one, the one giving the strength instead of accepting it. "Dylan, please hold my hand." She stretched her arm across the distance, knowing his reluctance to comply had nothing to do with her. He finally put his fingers in her palm tentatively, his arm tensed for immediate withdrawal. She covered them with her other hand, then leaned forward, bracing herself with their clasped hands on his knee. "What happened upstairs frightened me a little, too." When he would have pulled his hand away, she tightened her grasp. "I didn't expect it, either. All at once, I'm looking forward to our wedding day much more than I have before. But the simple fact we were tempted to go too far doesn't make our feelings for each other wrong."

"What if I hadn't realized what was happening soon enough? What if I had let things get out of hand?" Through the deepening dusk, she saw his brows knit in distress.

"Honey, there were two of us up there. I know you want to take care of me, to protect me, but I'm not a child. If we'd let passion take over, it would have been as much my choice as yours. The reality is we decided together to draw the line."

He still sat firmly on his side of the seat, holding himself away from her. His gaze traveled from the hand she refused to release, over her shoulder and out the window.

"Dylan, please look at me." The pain in his eyes made her want to gather him into a hug, but she knew it wouldn't be wise. "Please don't beat yourself up over this, and please, double please, don't shut me out because you're afraid of what might happen. Now we know it's not a good idea for us to be alone together in your apartment. So we go other places for our dates. Engagement is the time where we learn to work as a team, and that includes discovering and avoiding situations which aren't good for us together. We can't learn to be a team if you pull away because of what might happen."

Ever so slowly, she saw the shadows in his eyes move away. They sat for what may have been hours or minutes, watching thoughts and feelings cross each other's faces. Leslie knew she'd won when his fingers tightened around hers. "God definitely knew what he was doing when He made you part of my heart, Leslie-love. Your wisdom takes my breath away." He lifted her hand to his lips and slowly bestowed a kiss on it, his gaze never leaving her eyes. Tears filled his eyes, creating a similar response in hers. "I feel like we've been through a war and only emerged alive because we stuck together."

"That's what being a team is all about." She returned his watery smile.

He twisted around into driving position and tugged at his hand. "If you'll let me have my hand back, I'll find us a steak dinner with which to celebrate."

four

They drove in silence to the Ranchlands Dining Room, Nipson's nicest eating establishment. It was a healing, comforting silence, similar to the stillness after a thunderstorm. Once he'd helped her from the car, Dylan held his elbow at an awkward angle from his side. "May I escort you, m'lady?" His vulnerable expression turned the playful words into a plea for reassurance.

"With pleasure, sir." Leslie put her hand on the inside crook of his arm.

The hostess seemed to take their measure immediately and escorted them to a table partially concealed by large plants. Once the bustle of bringing menus and water, reciting the specials, and taking their order had passed, they sat looking at each other as if searching for clues as to what to say next.

"Are you hiding?" she finally asked.

He took a long sip of water. "I don't know. I feel like I'm in one of those huge canvas balls they set up for kids at carnivals where you walk around inside on a massive air cushion. The more people who are in there with you, the harder it is to walk. The only way to keep from falling over is to stand still."

"I never went inside one of those, but I know what you mean." She pondered her next thought carefully before speaking. "Don't you think this next year, maybe the next two years, will be like this a lot of the time? You'll have new responsibilities at the church, while I have new challenges at home. Even after we're married, it will take time to adjust to the way circumstances will change our relationship."

"I guess I never thought of it that way before. It scares me to think of all the ways in which I can make mistakes which will end up hurting you."

"As long as we're working it through together, I'll be fine. The only thing which will hurt me past enduring is if something separates us in spirit. If we make a point of telling each other honestly how we're feeling and what we're thinking, that won't happen."

"I promise." He held his right hand across the table as if to seal his words with a handshake.

She gripped his hand firmly. "I do, too."

He winked at her. "Have you ever thought you might have missed your calling? Based on the last sixty minutes, I'd say you would make an awesome marriage counselor."

She shook her head. "I couldn't begin to tell other people how to manage their lives. Just my own is enough."

"How about an interior decorator, then? I believe we were discussing it when we got distracted."

"Hmmm." She pretended to consider. "That's not technically in my job description for the next ten months, but I might make an exception for a special case."

"How special?"

The waitress appeared with a steaming plate in each hand. "Here's your garlic shrimp, ma'am, and a medium well steak for you, sir. Would either of you care for anything else?"

"Just water refills, please," Dylan requested.

Once the water glasses had been replenished and the waitress had retreated again, they bowed their heads for Dylan to ask a quick blessing over the food. He then looked up with a mischievous grin. "You haven't answered my question."

"I've been thinking it over so I can make an informed decision." She had to work to keep the giggle out of her voice. His recovering spirits gave her a giddy feeling of relief. "Since you're the nicest looking man around, and since you're buying my dinner, I think you'll qualify as a special case."

"Who said anything about buying dinner?" he protested, though his affectionate smile reassured her.

She dipped a plump shrimp into cocktail sauce. "Do you have any household items at all?"

"Just what you saw and several boxes of books."

"I'm sure we have some linens we could loan you, and probably some extra dishes." Mentally she sorted through each of the cupboards at home. "We might be able to find some decent drapes at a garage sale."

"Or we could go shopping for some together as our first purchase for our new home." The thought appeared to have cheered him immensely.

Her own excitement threatened to squelch her appetite. "That would be fun." Then another thought sobered her. "I'm afraid I don't have any money to contribute, though. Registration for this next semester of school took almost all my savings."

"Then I'll buy them, with your help of course, and when I say in my wedding vows that 'all my worldly goods I thee endow,' you'll know exactly what you're getting."

Laughter almost made her choke on the water she'd just sipped. "Maybe I should revise the vows to exclude the Princess."

He leaned away from his empty plate with a hurt expression. "Oh my wounded pride! How could you be so cruel?"

"Just heartless, I guess." She shrugged carelessly, delighted to see his goofy humor functioning again. "But back to the interior decorating, or should I say lack thereof. Why don't you spend the next couple of nights at our house until we get your apartment in living condition?"

For a moment, she thought he'd surrender to guilt-induced objections, but finally he nodded. "If you're sure it won't inconvenience anyone, it would be treat for me. Frankly, the idea of going back to that place tonight has less than no appeal."

Mentally she reached for a way to steer the conversation in a different direction. "Have you found any time for job-hunting?"

"As a matter of fact, I didn't have to search very hard. When I talked to Pastor Quillan last Saturday, he said he'd heard of an opening at the sawmill. He put in an application for me, and on Wednesday they called to say the job is mine."

"How much notice do you have to give at the rig?"

"I offered them fourteen days last weekend, but they found a replacement who was willing to start right away. So here I am."

"Dessert?" the waitress offered, lifting their empty plates off the table.

Leslie checked Dylan's face, then shook her head. "Not for me, thanks."

"Me either," Dylan said, then leaned forward when the waitress was out of earshot and whispered, "Since I've already been invited to your house, I thought I'd take a risk on there being some leftover oatmeal cake."

She laughed. "And if there's not?"

"I'll have to speak to your dad about being such a glutton, or would it be Vince?"

His question brought back the worry she'd been dodging. "Actually, Vince isn't home much."

Spontaneously, he reached for her hand. "What's happening?"

She told about Dr. Wallace's concern for Andrew, Andrew's response, and what she'd been observing during the week. Several minutes later she concluded with, "I'm trying not to assume responsibility for either of them, but it hurts to watch. Andrew needs all the encouragement he can get, but Vince can't, or maybe won't, give it. For some reason, he's withdrawing from us, too. I have this feeling again that my family's falling apart and there's nothing I can do about it."

"You've come a long way to be able to recognize there's nothing you can do." Gentleness filled both his expression and his voice. "But in some ways it makes the heartache worse."

Her throat clogged with unreleased emotion. "I'd hoped Andrew's accident was the end of the book for us. If that didn't scare him away from drinking, nothing will. Vince appeared to adopt a different attitude that night, but his reformation doesn't look any more permanent than Andrew's. I just wish I knew why God lets the struggles continue."

"I know." The rest of his reply came slowly, after a long hesitation. "I could give you several glib, spiritual sounding explanations, but I doubt any of them are even related to the truth. I think only God Himself can answer accurately, though in my experience, 'why' is a question He seems to prefer to leave unanswered." His contemplative gaze moved from their joined hands back to her face, picking up an admiring smile on the way. "I can tell you this with certainty. You've changed a lot in the last few months."

"In a good way, I hope." Her gaze clung to his, accepting the silent strength he offered.

His expression turned reminiscent. "Several years ago, a pair of eagles built a nest near one of the camps where I worked. Every evening, I'd sneak over to their tree to watch what they were doing. Sure enough, three little ones eventually hatched out. I spent hours watching them learn to fly. Two caught on right away, but the third one just couldn't seem to get it. His parents would push him out of the nest, screeching and squawking. He'd flap his stubby little wings frantically without gaining any momentum. One of the parents would eventually dive under him, lift him back to the nest, and start the process all over. I'll never forget the day he learned simply to spread his wings and let the air currents lift him. I felt as proud of him as if I'd taught him myself. You remind me of that eagle, Leslie-love. You've learned how to let the winds of family struggle lift you. Four months ago, you would have been incapable of enjoying an evening with me, knowing your brothers were at odds. Tonight, you're using the frustration as a springboard for finding out more about your Heavenly Father."

"Thanks." His compliment warmed her through. "I just wish this were a test like we get at school. Take it once, and you're finished."

He nodded his understanding, then softly asked, "Are you in any hurry to get home? I'd like to take a drive."

Her emotions had steadied enough to let her tease, "What about the oatmeal cake?"

He grinned smugly while placing money under the bill that their waitress had brought on a minute tray. "I happen to be on excellent terms with the official oatmeal cake baker in Nipson. I'm sure she'd whip up another one just for me if the other one doesn't last until we get there."

"You're terribly sure of yourself," she warned, slipping her hand under his arm as they left the restaurant.

He waited to answer until they were both seated in the car. "No, just sure of her."

"I'm glad." She slid over to the middle of the seat. Once he had the car started, his arm came around her shoulders to keep her close. They drove aimlessly around the darkened countryside for more than an hour, recalling special memories and discussing what the next months might hold. He had just turned the car back toward town when she peered up at the sky, then requested softly, "Please stop, Dylan. There's the northern lights."

The streaks of light were in just the right place for the couple to watch without getting out of the car. No colors showed up tonight, just gently undulating, glowing swaths across the sky. He hugged her tighter to his shoulder. "Do you remember what happened the first time we watched the northern lights together?"

She turned her head to face him in the shadows. "You told me you loved me."

"We did this for the first time, too." He dipped his head for a quick kiss. "While we've been driving around, I've been thinking a lot about some of the things you said earlier this evening. I'm glad you said what you did." His silence felt heavy with unspoken thoughts.

"Can you elaborate?"

His smile reached her through the darkness. "Until tonight, I haven't fully appreciated your strength. We met at a time when you needed someone to augment that strength, and my ego loved the feeling of always being there for you, even standing between you and difficulties when I could. I started seeing myself as some kind of Superman in your world. Earlier this evening, I showed myself just how human I am. I had to face the fact I can't build an idyllic world for you, because even I'm capable of causing problems in it. When I just about let myself get swamped in self-pity, you refused to let it happen. After seeing my weakness, you once again trusted me with your burdens. I've known I needed you because I love you. Tonight I realized I need you because you're my balance. You're not just an addition to my life that makes me feel strong and macho. You're a necessary part of my soul."

She sat quietly in his embrace, pondering how to reply. His ragged honesty filled her to bursting with loving admiration. "Probably every girl dreams of a modern version of the white knight. You were my white knight this spring. If you hadn't been around, I might have become a victim of my own compulsions. Even tonight, you helped me find strength to continue coping with what's happening at home. Yet while it's nice to be on the receiving end, it's great to be able to give, too. A romantic storybook would have you going ahead of me in life, slaying all my dragons for me, but I'd rather walk beside you. We'll do a better job on the dragons if we do it together."

five

A soft tapping on her bedroom door awoke Leslie the next morning. "Yeah?" she croaked sleepily.

"It's me, the love of your life. I thought you might like to go for an early morning walk."

Just the sound of his voice brought her wide awake. "I'll be ready in fifteen minutes."

She slouched on the edge of her bed for several moments, an involuntary smile spreading itself across her face. Dad and Mum had both been delighted when she had brought Dylan home last night and announced his need of a place to stay for a couple of days.

"Of course we don't mind," Mum assured him with the gracious manner Leslie admired. Her tone implied Dylan was doing them a favor by staying. "Tomorrow afternoon, Leslie and I can go through the closets around here. I doubt you'll need much more than what we have just taking up space."

Leslie's thoughts moved on to the day ahead. Sounds from downstairs indicated Dad was already up making breakfast. Church would be next on the agenda, then lunch and another Carlson tradition called family council, which meant a gathering in the family room. Sometimes Dad called family council to discuss a specific problem. This afternoon's meeting just meant one last afternoon together before Vince returned to university in Bayfield. Another church service in the evening would conclude the day. Yet throughout each part of the busyness, Dylan would be there.

47

With a smile, she quickly washed her face and brushed her teeth, then pulled on a pair of warm socks, jeans, and a heavy white sweatshirt printed in falling leaf patterns. A scrunchie secured her hair in a ponytail. Her running shoes were downstairs on the shelf in the entry way. Dylan met her at the door, her light jacket in his hands.

"It's a bit crisp out this morning," he informed her, letting his hands linger on her shoulders after settling her jacket into place.

She took note of his wind-mussed hair and reddened cheeks. "You've already been out?"

He closed the door behind them and draped his arm over her shoulders. "I woke up early, so decided to wander around for a bit. It wasn't much fun without you, so I got you up, then sat out here on the swing while I waited."

"Are you nervous about church?"

They had walked almost a full block away from the house before he answered. "I think so." His grin flashed a hint of embarrassment. "The first month of any new job is awkward. If anything, this is worse because it's a ministry as well as a job. Does that make any sense?"

She nodded, wrapping her arm around his waist. "Being part of a pastoral staff is different from anything you've done so far."

"It also means a different kind of relationship with people than either of us has experienced."

"What do you mean?"

"You've grown up in Heritage Christian Assembly. While many people have high regard for you, you're still one of the kids. I joined the Assembly as a Bible school student, so I'm also one of the younger generation. As soon as my new position is announced, we're both going to be under scrutiny as people move us from the kid category to the leadership pedestal."

"Why would they put either of us on a pedestal?" She looked at him questioningly. "Pastor Quillan has always worked hard at making us understand he's our servant, rather than our dictator. You're no different."

"That's one of the reasons I feel so privileged to be able to work with him." He grimaced. "Unfortunately, some people have a need to idolize others in leadership. They confuse responsibility with power, and develop expectations for those they see as powerful."

"That's dumb." For the first time, Leslie wanted to hide from Dylan's new job.

He chuckled. "It is, but then humans aren't always as intelligent as they like to think. The positive side of these changes, though, is that we'll get to know Pastor and Mrs. Quillan in a different way, too."

"How so?"

"How well do you know the Quillans?"

"Not that well. I think my dad and the pastor are pretty good friends, but I've never had an opportunity to know them as anything but my pastor and his wife."

"My point exactly." His triumphant grin brought an answering smile to her face. "Pastor Quillan and I will now be coworkers. Though I hope to learn a lot from him, I also hope to learn about him, the kind of man he is inside, what he's experienced in his life to make him the kind of person he is. I'd also like to learn about Mrs. Quillan, the hard parts and the enjoyable parts of being a pastor's wife and how I can make that job easier for you. Since we're a team, you'll be learning right along with me."

Her stomach felt fluttery at the thought. She'd never before thought about the changes and expectations that would come to her as part of Dylan's ministry. All at once, she felt compelled to gain as much from Mrs. Quillan's experience as possible.

Uncertainty still tightened her nerves later in the morning as she entered Heritage Christian Assembly arm in arm with Dylan. Though the congregation didn't know about his new position yet, she already felt on display. Pastor Quillan, a solidly built man a few inches shorter than Dylan with gray hair and perceptive dark eyes, met them at the door. He shook Leslie's hand first, then Dylan's. "Good morning. I trust you settled in successfully yesterday, Dylan."

"Actually, I'm still in the process. The Carlsons are generously supplying me with just about everything."

"Good." He lowered his voice. "Rather than announcing your new job right away, I thought I'd wait a couple of weeks. It should also give you time to get comfortable in your job at the mill and in your new apartment. Does that sound okay with you?"

"I appreciate it, Pastor Quillan."

"That's the other thing." The pastor looked decidedly uncomfortable. "I know people like me to carry around a title, but I'd really rather not. I compromise by asking folks to call me Pastor Jim. It seems to satisfy their need for a respectful label and mine for informality." He beckoned to a short, plump lady with a gentle smile. "This is my wife, Theresa."

She tucked one hand under her husband's arm and extended the other in welcome. "As soon as you get settled, we'd like to have you both over for dinner." Her burgundy coat dress accentuated the whiteness of her hair, which she'd pulled back in a sleek chignon. Her blue eyes studied Leslie, then seemed to soften with approval. "I'm looking forward to getting better acquainted with you both."

"Thank you." Leslie hoped her short reply didn't sound terse. The older couple moved on to greet others.

"They didn't make you nervous, did they?" Dylan teased softly, as they made their way into the sanctuary.

"I know they shouldn't, but it was like meeting them for the first time," she admitted. "I feel like if I do or say the wrong thing, it will reflect badly on you."

"You'll do fine." He reassured her with a smile, then followed her into the row where her parents and brothers had already found seats. As happened every Sunday, Brad, Karen, and the baby joined them.

"Good morning." Karen greeted them brightly in the tone Leslie recognized as her "Sunday morning voice."

Mum held out her arms for her grandson, who pitched himself into them with a delighted, "Gama!"

The church's small orchestra struck up a peppy chorus, precluding any further conversation. It didn't take Leslie long to abandon her unhappy thoughts and focus on the worship now filling the sanctuary. A majestic choir presentation made her promise herself to resume the weekly practices she'd abandoned after Andrew's accident. She glanced over at him on the other side of Mum. For some reason, he still preferred sitting with his family to joining the church group his age. Worry niggled at her, but she pushed it away to concentrate on the sermon.

It didn't take Karen long after the service ended to pull Leslie aside. "Has Vince said anything to you about Andrew?"

Leslie forced down a feeling of defensiveness. "He's been so busy with work he hasn't been home much."

Karen smiled at her as one would at a small child. "He hasn't been as busy as he wanted you to think. He's been out at the farm quite a bit."

"Why didn't he want us to know where he was?" Leslie tried to keep her tone neutral.

"Dad hasn't been as understanding of Vince as he might have been. Vince says he feels like the one who's created the problems, instead of Andrew."

A multitude of questions clamored through Leslie's mind, but she firmly refused to give any of them voice. To her immense relief, Li'l Brad toddled over with Mum close behind and Karen's train of thought changed abruptly. "Have you noticed how well he's walking? I almost can't keep up to him anymore." She scooped her son up into a hug, then tickled him under his chin to make him laugh.

Leslie slipped away from the trio. How she wished Karen would take her complaints directly to their parents rather than saddling Leslie with them! Dylan approached with her Bible and purse. "I was getting ready to ride in on my white steed to rescue you, but the little ankle-biter did it for me. Are you ready to leave?"

She nodded. "I'm giving thanks Karen didn't invite herself to this afternoon's family council."

"Should I hang around for the meeting or make myself scarce?" He held one of the double doors open for her.

"I don't think Dad would mind your staying, and I'd be relieved to have you there."

"For a particular reason, or just for my charming company?" He glanced at her with a grin before carefully guiding the car out of the parking lot which teemed with darting youngsters.

She took a deep breath. "Apparently Vince has been talking with Brad and Karen about his frustrations with the family. I'm not sure whether I want him to talk with us about them or pretend everything's okay. I'm just getting tired of the unending conflict. If it's not one family member, it's another." Brightening her tone, she added, "Your charming company will make everything easier."

Gently taking her hand, he only said, "I'm glad."

Lunch lived up to Leslie's fondest hopes for a mellow, comfortable Sunday afternoon meal. "Your fried chicken was delicious as usual," Dad complimented her, pushing back his plate. "Dessert looks even better. Are you sure I have to share it with Dylan and Vince?"

Leslie laughed. "I dare you to try keeping Dylan away from his favorite cake."

"You really need to start practicing self-restraint, old friend," Vince informed Dylan. "You could get chubby when you start eating my sister's cooking full time."

"I'll worry about that when the time comes," Dylan retorted. "For now, I want my fair share of that cake!"

Finally Dad pushed back from the table. "This has been an exceptionally nice Sunday dinner. Thanks, Leslie. Mum and I will clean up, and then we'd like to see everyone in the family room in about an hour."

"I'd like to get packed so I can leave by five." Though Vince used a conversational tone, his eyes reflected an arrogance that startled Leslie.

Dad's tone also stayed casual, but he met his son's gaze squarely. "We won't take up more of your afternoon than is necessary, son."

Vince left the dining area with a scowl. Dad watched him, frown lines deepening between his eyes. Mum squeezed his hand. He looked at her, and his expression softened. Unspoken communication passed between them before they began clearing the table.

Leslie looked across the table to find Dylan watching her. He stood and silently gestured toward the family room. When she reached toward two bowls of food, Dad cleared his throat loudly. His raised eyebrows and the straight line of his mouth communicated the same kind of no-nonsense authority he'd shown Vince. As soon as she backed away from the table, his expression softened into a smile. "Good girl," he whispered as she passed.

In the family room, Dylan tugged two large beanbags close to the cold fireplace. "I wish I had a nickel for every time I've daydreamed in the last four months about sitting here with you." He plumped down on one bag and draped his arm across the other invitingly.

Snuggled into his half hug, Leslie felt ready to face anything. "I've missed it, too," she whispered, turning to look up into his face.

"Do you want to talk about why you're dreading this family council?" The compassion in his eyes told her he already understood, but he wanted to listen if she felt like talking.

"I'd hoped this afternoon could be just a friendly family chat," she admitted. "First Karen tells me how upset Vince is, and then he challenges Dad over something purely trivial. I wish he'd tell us why he's so upset."

"Maybe he feels threatened," Dylan offered.

"By what?"

"The changes in your family. Your mum isn't the sad, sickly woman she was six months ago. Andrew's walking a fine line between recovery and relapse. Meanwhile, more of your attention is focused on me than on Vince. He's accustomed to being your hero, you know."

"I know." She grinned wryly. "Unfortunately, he's tarnished his hero-image a fair bit this year."

"Don't be too hard on him," Dylan cautioned. "He's having to do some growing up, and that's never easy."

Andrew limped into the room, cutting off further private

conversation. "Hi, guys." He grinned and lowered himself onto the couch.

"How's the leg feeling?" Dylan asked.

"Pretty good most of the time. My muscles are still weak, so it gets tired easily. But Dr. Wallace predicts a couple of months of heavy physio can have me ready for basketball season in November."

"If you can stay away from the booze that long." Vince's biting comment preceded his appearance.

Andrew flushed, but Dad's voice from the hallway pre-empted any reply he might have made. "Vincent, your re-mark was inappropriate." Mum sat on the couch, close enough to Andrew to lay her hand reassuringly on his knee. Dad settled into the large easy chair by the door before continuing. "Do you have something you'd like to discuss with the family as the reason for your attitude?"

A mask of hardness imprinted itself on Vince's face. "You said yourself Dr. Wallace is concerned about Andrew's addiction, yet no one in this house has admitted out loud it's still a problem. You should know by now a problem like this doesn't go away just because you ignore it."

Dad sent a smile Andrew's direction. "There's a differ-ence between ignoring a problem and giving someone you love the benefit of the doubt. Andrew hasn't done anything since he left the hospital to arouse suspicion. Besides, Dr. Wallace clearly described for him the possibly fatal re-sponse his body could have to alcohol in the future. Andrew's enough of a man to be able to make a wise choice."

"Dr. Wallace told me to avoid any kind of alcohol, and I'm sure it will be no problem," Andrew supplied quickly, giving Mum a carefree grin.

His glib tone worried Leslie, as did Vince's derisive snort.

Anger flashed in Andrew's eyes, but before he could re-tort, Dad advised, "Don't dignify that with a reaction, Andrew. Vincent, you need to heed what Jesus told the Pharisees. 'Let him without sin cast the first stone.'" Vince's face flushed angrily, but Dad didn't give him a chance to speak.

"Andrew isn't the only one facing an unconquered prob-lem. I recall a similar meeting last spring in which we dis-cussed your holier-than-thou attitude toward your younger brother. Frankly, it's getting more than a little tiring. You claim to be so much more mature, but I have yet to see you demonstrate either forgiveness or compassion. Maybe you should spend less time criticizing and more time asking your Heavenly Father to work on your heart."

Vince gave no answer, but neither did he storm out of the room as he'd done in the past. After a couple of mo-ments of silence, Dad suggested each person name a per-sonal growth goal for the next four months, and the con-versation shifted into a more pleasant tone. When the meet-ing concluded, Vince even lingered to participate in a board game. Perhaps a truce had been reached this afternoon, but Leslie wondered how long it would last.

six

Dylan started at the mill the next day, and he left his apartment keys with Leslie so she could put the dishes and linens away for him. She also found a clock to hang on his kitchen wall, as well as a couple of wall decorations for his living area. A look through some boxes in the Carlson garage revealed a bedspread woven in a plaid of earth tones and a pair of beige throw pillows. On a Saturday visit to Nipson's only drapery shop, she found a swatch of fabric in exactly the shade of moss green she had envisioned.

"I can't picture what the finished product will look like," Dylan admitted, "but if this is what you want, it looks good to me."

The clerk wrote down the measurements Leslie gave her, then punched a few numbers into the calculator. When she quoted the cost for the fabric as well as sewing, Leslie looked at Dylan in shock. "Maybe I should sew them myself," she whispered.

He shook his head. "Not with your studies. This is about what I figured it would cost." He looked at the clerk. "When will they be ready?"

"Probably in about six weeks. Shall we give you a call?"

"Sure. I don't have a phone yet, so we'll give you hers." He recited Leslie's phone number effortlessly. Do you need a deposit?"

"Fifty percent is our policy."

After Dylan wrote the check, they thanked the clerk and left the store. A cool wind, typical of the time of the year,

57

caused Leslie to pull her jacket zipper all the way up. "Are you sure those won't be too expensive? We could have chosen a cheaper kind of fabric."

Once they were in the car, he turned to look at her directly. "Don't worry about it, Les. I've saved a bit from working at the rigs." His teasing grin reassured her more than his words. "What I make at the mill will be enough for me to live on, so my savings are all yours to spend as you like for our home. We probably won't have a large budget after we're married and into full time church work, so we'd do well to buy nice things now when we have the money. We'll be enjoying them for a long time."

Bible school classes started just two days later. The first day left Leslie feeling bereft. Just three months earlier, Dylan had accompanied her everywhere. Now he'd moved on, and she had a year's worth of education to acquire on her own. She wondered several times during the day why this final year held such importance in Dad's and Dylan's thinking. It felt to her like a waste of time, not to mention an inexplicable delay for what she wanted most. Tears felt close to the surface throughout the opening chapel service and the various class orientation sessions. To her dismay, she discovered James Trindle in almost every classroom she entered.

"What a pleasant surprise to find you here, Miss Carlson," he proclaimed when they ended up side by side in New Testament Studies. "I'd heard you were dropping out to get married. I'm glad to see you reconsidered that foolish decision."

She answered with a mere smile, not trusting herself to speak. She knew he hadn't heard any such rumor, though he'd probably tried to start it. He seemed to view himself as an expert on all matters of Christian behavior, while appearing oblivious to his own reputation as a notorious gossip.

When the class was dismissed, he made sure he exited the room beside her. "Are you by any chance headed for Christian Philosophy? What a coincidence. I am, too. So did you postpone your wedding or call it off entirely?"

She breathed deeply, willing herself to think clearly. "Neither. Dylan and I decided last spring we wouldn't get married until after I graduate."

Completely unrebuffed, he smiled indulgently. "I imagine you had a hard time persuading him to let you do that."

"Actually, it was his idea." She tried to move down the hall quickly enough to leave him behind. Threading her way through the crowd, she collided with a person headed just as quickly in the opposite direction. Her texts and notebooks scattered on the floor.

"Oh, I'm sorry." The young man turned toward her with a horrified expression. "I didn't see you coming."

She looked up at the obviously freshman student with what she hoped was a reassuring smile. "It was my fault. I got in too much of a hurry."

"Here. Let me help." He bent down to stack the books.

"I believe the next new student orientation begins in the chapel in four minutes," James announced patronizingly. "I'll help the lady so you don't get a lateness mark the first day of school."

The young man blushed vibrant red to the roots of his rumpled hair and vanished in a flurry of mortification.

"James, that was completely uncalled for." Leslie's wrath boiled out. "If you hadn't been hounding me, I wouldn't have run into that fellow in the first place."

Again, he smiled indulgently. "In any kind of accident between a lady and a gentleman, it's always the gentleman's fault. Here are your books, Miss Carlson."

His phony manners had always irritated her past endurance. "Thank you," she snapped, grabbing the stack from his hands.

He captured her left hand and studied the third finger intently. "Wow, that's quite a piece of jewelry. Is it a family heirloom?"

"No." She snatched her hand back. "It's my engagement ring."

"I never would have suspected Dylan could afford such an extravagant ring. It seems almost overdone, considering his pastoral aspirations, don't you think?"

Thankfully, the door to her destination appeared at her right, saving her the need to answer. "He's just so smug," she fumed to Dylan later that evening as they sat in the family room playing Scrabble. "He has no clue how totally irritating he is. Even more frustrating, he's in almost every class I'm taking this semester. I don't think I can tolerate an entire year of him. It makes me wonder again why I'm postponing what I really want for a degree I don't want."

Dylan's hand stopped suspended over the tile he had been about to place on the board. "Come again?"

She grinned and shrugged. "You and Dad thought it important I finish my Bible school degree, so I didn't argue. But I still don't understand why the degree is so important. Having a Bachelor of Arts is like having a Bachelor of Basketweaving. It means nothing in the job market."

"A Bachelor of Biblical Studies isn't all bad." He finally finished placing his word and pulled his hand back.

"I'm not saying it is. It just has no practical value beyond the discipline of four years of study."

Genuine perplexity clouded his gaze. "I know I men-

tioned things being tight financially after we get into the
pastorate full time, but I didn't mean to make you feel you
had to bring in an income, too."

"I know." She softened her voice soothingly. "But if I
did have to get a job, what skills do I have? What if something happens to you after we have a family?"

"Hey, I'm not planning to do anything stupid and get
myself into trouble. I plan to be around long enough to
have you push me in a wheelchair up and down the halls of
the old folks' home."

"But what if that plan doesn't work out? I just feel like I
ought to have more to show for this year than a piece of
paper that doesn't really mean anything." She held his gaze
with her own, willing him to understand her point of view.

"Do you have something specific in mind?"

"Today, during Dad's philosophy orientation session, an
idea did occur to me. I think Dean Williams might let me
challenge Philosophy 401. If I don't know Dr. Carlson's
Christian philosophy by now, I don't think I'll ever get it.
Then I'd like to write for a copy of Bayfield University's
extension catalogue and talk with the Dean about what
courses I'd need to take to upgrade from an Arts to a Science degree, with an emphasis on business. It would take
some cooperation between the Bible school and the university, but the university has been advertising that they
want to develop a long distance degree program. Do you
think it's worth a try?"

He stared at the abandoned game for a long time, but
when he met her gaze again his eyes held the affectionate
encouragement she craved. "When I get my ego out of the
way, I think it's a terrific idea. If you're finishing your
degree simply to please your dad and me, then we'd be
foolish to try to discourage you from doing something which

would make it meaningful to you. I am worried, though, about the amount of work involved. You're sure you won't wear yourself out?"

"I won't know until the Dean and I talk about it. He might even decide the idea just isn't practical."

But Dean Williams endorsed her plan heartily. "I'd like to see more of our women students acquire non-church related skills. I'll talk with Bayfield's Dean of Academics to get their approval and look over your transcript for the last three years to see what courses you can drop from our regular requirements to give you time for as heavy a load as the university might demand."

When Leslie and Dylan accepted Pastor Jim and Theresa's dinner invitation a couple of evenings later, the older couple also applauded her goal. "I've met too many pastors' wives whose entire living experience has taken place in the church," Theresa commented. "They have no way of relating to the women in their congregations who work outside the home or haven't grown up in Christian families."

"If Dylan gets called to a city church," Pastor Jim added, "you'll be surprised at the respect people will have for him because of your education."

Their gracious manner made Leslie feel enough at ease to voice her thoughts. "I'm still intimidated by how what I do or say can affect Dylan's ministry. What people think of me will influence how they respond to him."

"Only if they let it," Theresa replied firmly. "It took me several years into our ministry to realize what other people think of me and of Jim is their responsibility and between them and God. We started out trying so hard to please everyone we almost lost our marriage."

Pastor Jim reached across the corner of the table for his

wife's hand. "It was then I realized all the approval in the world couldn't replace Theresa. We promised each other we wouldn't let anyone or anything become more important to us than our marriage. Forty years later, we're still at it."

"So what's the balance between not offending people and being over-influenced by their opinion?" Leslie wondered aloud. She noticed how Pastor Jim looked to his wife for the response.

She smiled sympathetically at the younger couple. "Unfortunately, ministry isn't like a business where you provide a specific service in a timely and friendly manner and all your customers are happy. Ministry is a matter of relationships—the way you relate with the congregation both individually and collectively, how the people relate with one another, how the church fits into the community, and mostly each person's relationship with God. As I'm sure you've discovered, any relationship becomes a breeding ground for misunderstanding unless everyone involved actively works at prevention. Sometimes you find a church like Heritage where the majority of the church family sees the health of the family as everyone's responsibility. Other times, you find yourself in situations where the congregation seems determined to make the pastor's job as difficult as possible. Because you're always dealing with people, and people are generally unpredictable, there's no way to guarantee not offending them."

Pastor Jim continued the explanation. "The only effective guideline we've found is our motive. If our choice of action or words is based in doing what we feel before God we're supposed to do or say, then other people's objections are their own problem. However, if we've acted in self-defense or for other selfish reasons, we have to ask forgiveness of those we've offended." He looked at the young couple and chuckled. "You two remind me of Theresa and myself in our early days together. I was ready to wade into any church, any situation, and make whatever difference I could. The mere idea thoroughly intimidated my wife. Your expression, Leslie, is exactly the one I used to see on her face at least every Sunday and several times during the week."

Dylan squeezed Leslie's hand reassuringly. "In the last year, Leslie's experienced the best and the worst of what a church family can offer. I'm still not sure I did her any favor by interning in her home church."

Leslie would have preferred to let one of the Quillans respond, but both of them appeared to be waiting for her answer. "If I let my uncertainties stop me, I never would have agreed to marry you. No matter where you intern or pastor, we'd both still have the same lessons to learn. If you'd chosen differently, we'd be separated until next summer and then I'd have to get used to being a pastor's wife along with adjusting to an unfamiliar place and people I didn't know. At least here we both have people we love and trust we can turn to and we're learning together."

Both of the Quillans were smiling broadly by the time she finished. Theresa simply nodded encouragingly at her, while Pastor Jim directed his comments to Dylan. "One of my biggest challenges as a pastor has been keeping my perspective, making sure insignificant problems don't take up more of my thoughts than the truly important matters. I see indications of the same trait in you, and Leslie is exactly the balance you need. If you'll let yourself lean on her as much as you try to protect her, her outlook will keep you focused in the right direction."

Dylan's sheepish grin told Leslie he was remembering

their conversation his first night back in town. "You don't know how right you are, Pastor Jim. One of these days I hope I won't need to be reminded quite so often."

"Don't count on it." Pastor Jim started stacking empty plates. "Even after forty years of marriage, I still try to be Superman for Theresa, forgetting that in many ways she's far stronger than I. How do you feel about helping me with dishes?"

"I'd be glad to." Dylan pushed back from the table. "I fell in love with Leslie over a sink full of soapy water."

Theresa laughed. "Now there's a romantic environment! How about a walk, Leslie?"

Dusk had already begun to settle in as they stepped outside. "Every fall I'm surprised by how quickly the days shorten," Leslie observed. "In only another month or so, it will be dark before suppertime."

"I know what you mean," Theresa agreed. Though a good six inches shorter than Leslie, her stride kept her companion moving quickly. "We first moved to Nipson from down south along the coast about this time of year. During that first winter, I had a tough battle with depression. Between having only a few hours of daylight each day and the snow covering everything, the world looked bleakly monochromatic. When your mother started struggling with depression the next year, I had a lot more compassion for her than I might have had otherwise."

"Did you know Mum well before she got sick?" Leslie stuffed her hands into her jacket pockets against the chill of the evening wind.

"Pretty well, I think. When your dad and Jim would have board meetings, I'd go over to your house and visit with your mum. As I used to help get you bathed and tucked in for the night, I never dreamed one day you'd be marrying my husband's assistant." Theresa put an arm around Leslie's waist. "I probably shouldn't say this, but I know you'll accept it with discretion. I've often thought in recent years you've probably grown up the best of the Carlson children. Maybe it was the responsibility of caring for Andrew, maybe it's just the kind of person you are. Your faith has expanded, especially in the last year, from a child's simple trust to a woman's confidence in who God is. I haven't a single doubt concerning your ability to cope with being in the ministry with Dylan."

The reassurance brought tears to Leslie's eyes. "It means a lot to hear you say so."

Theresa squeezed Leslie's waist, then also put her hands in her pockets. "Your mum and I used to talk about how we perceived our husbands as big men on the inside as well as the outside. They have a big faith, big dreams, and big hearts. We used to wonder if we were big enough inside ourselves to keep up with them. Your Dylan's the same kind of man, and I see the same question in your eyes when he talks about his calling. I wish I'd believed years ago what I'm about to tell you. God wouldn't have made us partners with them if we didn't have what it takes. Like Jim said tonight, we're strong in ways our big men aren't. Their bigness includes big vulnerabilities and sometimes our confidence in them is greater than their confidence in themselves."

Leslie turned to smile shakily at her. "Just in the last couple of weeks, I've discovered how much Dylan expects of himself and how unforgiving he is when he thinks he's failed."

Theresa nodded. "My Jim's the same way, and yet, if they didn't expect so much of themselves, they probably wouldn't accomplish as much as they do."

"I'll have to remember that."

"I'd like you to remember one other thing." Theresa stopped so she could look up into Leslie's face. "When things get hard, and they will, please don't be afraid to come talk with me. I've been where you are. I won't think any less of you or of Dylan because of anything you tell me. Hopefully, my mistakes will save you from a few. Will you consider me your friend?"

No words came readily, so Leslie simply embraced Theresa, knowing a hundred years wouldn't give her enough time to acquire this depth of wisdom and compassion.

seven

A week later, the tantalizing aroma of baked spareribs greeted her and Dad when they entered the house. Total silence indicated Mum must be napping. Leslie tiptoed down the hall to Andrew's room, where the door stood slightly ajar. She tapped softly.

"Yeah."

"It's me," Leslie whispered. "May I come in?"

"If you want." His taciturn responses were like painful echoes from this past spring.

She pushed the door open. He lay on his bed, staring at the ceiling, his injured leg propped up on a couple of pillows. "You okay, Andy?" Only she ever got away with using the nickname.

He didn't look at her. "Yeah."

She kept her tone gentle. "You don't sound like it."

"It's nothing against you, Les, but I'd rather be left alone."

"I'm just concerned about you."

"Don't be." The words came out sharply, then he actually turned toward her. "After four solid hours in physio, with people poking, pulling, and nattering at me, I need some quiet. I'll be fine."

Just as surely as she knew he hadn't told her the whole truth, she knew she wouldn't gain anything by insisting he talk. "I love you," she whispered, and left.

He didn't look much happier at the supper table. Even his favorite dessert, Mum's sinfully rich chocolate pie, elicited no more than a mumbled "thanks." He didn't try to duck out of doing dishes, though he said little, leaving conversation up to Dad and Leslie.

"Has Dean Williams heard anything from the university yet?" Dad wanted to know.

"He told me on Friday the University Dean of Academics appeared favorable to my plan on a test basis, but they're still working out the academic details. He figures it will take another couple of weeks at least." She snapped the lid firmly over a dish of leftover corn, which she then placed in the refrigerator.

"Does he see any problem with your being able to graduate in June?"

"Not so far. Next semester I will most likely be carrying a little more than a full load of university credits, but I shouldn't have to take anything at the Bible school and I'll be able to work at home." The ringing doorbell interrupted her.

Andrew's friend Tom stood grinning on the porch. "Hi, Leslie. Is Andrew home?"

"Sure." Leslie stood aside to let him in. "It's been awhile since we've seen you."

"Yeah." The teenager slouched awkwardly in the entry. "I just didn't see Andrew at school today, so I thought I'd find out if he's okay."

"He's in the kitchen." Leslie took his jacket and hung it in the closet. By the time she returned to the kitchen, Andrew and Tom had already vanished into Andrew's room. "Dad, did you hear Tom when he first came in?"

Dad nodded. "Andrew didn't look ready to supply any information, so I didn't press. I'll dig into it later. What's your plan for the evening?"

"Just some minor studying and probably an early bedtime.

Why?"

"No particular reason. I might see if Mum wants to start a game of something a bit later. If you're still up, a third person would be handy."

"So I'm merely handy," she teased. "It sounds like I'll have to call Dylan if I want any genuine appreciation."

Dad just grinned and disappeared down the hall. She went to the phone, then remembered Dylan had to work the graveyard shift this week. In other words, she'd have to wait until Saturday to talk with him. Squelching her disappointment, she spread out her class notes on the kitchen table. This way she'd be nearby if the others did decide to play a game, she explained mentally, then chided herself. *Be honest, Carlson. You don't want to miss anything when Tom and Andrew finally come out of hiding.* She forced herself to concentrate on the closely-written pages. Near the end of the third page, harsh voices caught her attention. She strained to make out words, but couldn't until the door opened. "Just butt out!" The sound of Andrew's rude command barely preceded Tom's hasty, pale-faced exit. She hurried to retrieve his jacket for him. By the time she'd closed the front door behind Tom, Andrew's bedroom door had closed again.

The following days didn't uncover any new causes for concern or bring reassurance, either. Thursday evening, she found herself in Dad's study, trying to find the right words to express her uneasiness. She started with a simple question as she handed Dad his cup of mocha. "Has Andrew told you why he missed school on Monday?"

"Not yet. Has he said anything to you?" His eyes twinkled with gentle amusement at her fretting.

"He won't talk to me."

He smiled compassionately. "Your chick is growing up,

Mother Hen."

Her cup of steaming instant cappuccino radiated comforting warmth. "I just can't help feeling something is wrong."

"I know." He nodded, then sipped his drink a couple of times. "I'm concerned about him, too. However, he's no longer a child we can protect. We have to leave him free to make mistakes and trust him to ask for our help when he wants it."

She tried to keep her voice steady. "It hurts to be shut out."

"Of course it does." His tone told her he truly understood. "But the alternative is having him dependent on you forever."

"I also wish Vince would call. It's been two weeks since he left."

"Maybe his silence means he's doing some serious thinking. It's not easy being forced to exchange self-righteousness for maturity."

"Dylan said something similar the afternoon Vince left. He has a lot more compassion for Vince than I do."

"Your fiancé faces problems more honestly than just about anyone I know. That kind of honesty lends itself readily to compassion."

She grinned at the praise for her love. "I feel guilty for saying so, but it's too bad Vince isn't more like Dylan."

"Maybe by the time he's Dylan's age, he will be." Dad swirled his drink in his cup, then took a large swallow. "Dylan has already experienced heartache in a way Vince is just discovering."

She nodded. Dylan's family had been through a crisis when he was in his late teens. He'd responded by running away. *But only for a time*, she mentally reminded herself.

Eventually he returned home, made peace with his family, and took up preparation for pastoral ministry. She grinned. "Sometimes I forget Dylan's had six more years of living than Vince has."

"Dylan's faith is also a solid part of who he is instead of a mask he wears to impress people." Dad's voice held no criticism for his son. "Maybe this is what my boy needs to show him how to be real with God as well as with himself."

The words made sense, but Leslie couldn't shake her feelings of brewing crisis. If only she could talk with Dylan. Though the wish crossed her mind, she refused to let it settle. He had signed up for the graveyard shift at the mill so he'd be available during afternoons and evenings at the church. She simply had to adjust to sharing his time with other responsibilities.

Friday brought good news from Dean Williams. The university had agreed to accept her as a long distance student on a trial basis for the current school year. "They've already indicated they'll take four or five students next year if this works well for you," he said, handing her a list of business management and computer science courses the university would require her to take. "It looks like we can reduce your Bible school credits to six, which leaves you two full days and three afternoons for your other studies. I've talked with the administration office about making a work station available to you during the afternoons for your computer courses, and Mrs. Tyler has said she'd welcome your help if you wanted to do your nine-week business practicum at the administration office, as well. Any questions?"

Leslie grinned at him. "Not yet. I still can't believe this is all working out so well. After I've studied the list overnight, I'll probably have three pages worth of questions."

He grinned back. "I've attached an outline of how your two programs of study will work together. Because of the extra work you did last year, it wouldn't take much for you to get a full Biblical Studies degree along with the Bachelor of Science from the university. If you'd like to study the proposal over the weekend, we can talk further about it Monday right after lunch."

She'd never even considered the possibility of a double major. "Thank-you, sir. It's a little much to absorb all at once."

"I'll give you one more thing to think about. Since you've paid registration for the entire year with us and will only be taking minimal credits, I'm planning to ask the rest of the administration if they would consent to the Bible school paying your university registration. I might even be able to persuade them to subsidize some of your courses since this is a pilot project which could have long-term benefit for us."

She left his office wanting to turn cartwheels down the hall. What he'd called a pilot project would make the difference between marking time and accomplishing something worthwhile. Scanning the list of requirements, she saw several that looked boring compared to Professor Jonas' theology class, for instance, but by the time she reached graduation, she'd have a diploma worth something in the job market. In addition, she probably wouldn't have to stretch her meager budget any further to pay for her goal.

James materialized in the hallway beside her. "You look happy, Miss Carlson." He made it sound like an infraction of some rule.

"Should I be unhappy about something?" She heard the

sarcasm in her tone, but he obviously didn't.

"Of course not. I only wondered if there's a specific reason for your happiness, so I can be happy with you." Even his laugh sounded patronizing.

Maybe if she changed the subject, she wouldn't feel so irritated. "It's unusual to see you wandering the halls during class time. Are you working on a special project?"

As she well knew, he never passed up an opportunity to talk about himself. "I actually just returned from an interview with Pastor Quillan. For the last several months, we've been working on a proposal I submitted to do my pastoral internship at Heritage. He told me he's been considering adding to the staff, so I'm pretty sure I have the job."

"I see." She wondered how Pastor Jim might describe the interview. More to the point, how would James react on Sunday when the pastor introduced Dylan as his assistant?

Leslie dreaded the announcement all weekend. As she explained to Dad, "I don't mind Dylan's new responsibilities, or even the fact I'll be associated with them. It's just the initial introduction, having to be the center of attention while people get used to the idea."

Dad just chuckled and squeezed her shoulders with reassurance.

She would have felt better if she could have talked with Dylan. Though she didn't try calling him until after lunch on Saturday to give him plenty of time to sleep, he'd already left his apartment. Resentment flashed through her at his choosing to spend his limited free time somewhere other than with her. Immediately she reprimanded herself. *You don't know this is free time for him. He might have a meeting with Pastor Jim.*

By the time she arrived at church with her family, she

felt on the edge of tears. Dylan hadn't appeared this morning to escort her, or even phoned to explain why he couldn't come. All her frustrations, uncertainties, and apprehensions were combining to make her world feel out of control.

He met her at the door with a hug. "Sorry I didn't make it this morning. I'll explain everything later."

Her resentment vanished as soon as she looked into his sparkling green eyes. He'd never deliberately ignore her. Just seeing him reminded her how much she loved him. So much, in fact, she could probably forgive him anything. "Will you be able to come over for the afternoon?"

He grinned apologetically. "Pastor Jim and Theresa wanted to take us out for lunch. Kind of a celebration, I think."

"Just the four of us, or will other people be there, too?" She hoped her nervousness didn't show.

"Just us four." With an arm around her shoulders, he guided her toward the pastor's study. "Pastor Jim and I wanted you with us for pre-service prayer." In the quiet hallway just outside the study, he stopped and turned to look directly into her eyes. "Leslie, this morning makes me feel like I'm stepping off a cliff. I know I'm called to be a pastor, but in the next few months I'm going to learn the hard way whether or not I have what it takes. I need to hear you tell me you're with me."

She studied his gaze for a few moments, then stood on tiptoe to place a gentle kiss on his lips. "Anything else you need to know?"

A glow of humor and affection replaced the previous uncertainty in his eyes. "I'd just like to confirm it." He tilted his head down toward her face.

An ostentatious throat clearing shattered the moment.

"Well!" James's scandalized tones echoed on the hall. "If this isn't a fine example for our young people."

Mingled embarrassment and indignation threatened to overload Leslie's already strained emotions, but Dylan's protective arm around her shoulders steadied her. "I don't see anyone in the area but you, James." His voice remained pleasant, despite its subtle edge. "If my love for my fiancée bothers you, it's not my problem."

A dull flush colored James' jawline. His eyes flashed anger, but he turned on his heel and disappeared around the corner.

Leslie wanted to tell Dylan about James's revelation on Friday, but he had already opened the door to Pastor Jim's study. The pastor and his wife sat on a couch along the opposite wall, holding hands.

"Welcome," Pastor Jim greeted Leslie. "Theresa and I have prayed together before every service since we started in the ministry. Since Dylan is now part of the team, we hope you'll join us, too, as often as you can."

"Thank you." She settled into the chair Dylan had pulled over from under the window on the left end of the office. He placed a second chair as close to hers as possible, then perched on the edge of it.

"I won't even ask if you're nervous," Pastor Jim told him with a smile. "Not only can I see it for myself, but I still remember my first Sunday. Let's ask for God's help maintaining His perspective." His prayer didn't last long, yet while he stated his request simply and gave thanks for the answer, Leslie felt Dylan relax. Even his grip on her hand loosened.

Ten minutes later, she entered the sanctuary hand-in-hand with him behind the older couple. She slipped into her usual seat beside Dad, while Theresa found a chair at the end of the second row across the aisle. Dylan and Pastor Jim took seats on the platform.

As soon as the organist and pianist finished their opening number, Pastor Jim stepped to the pulpit. "I sense rampant curiosity this morning." His blunt statement elicited a wave of laughter. "In answer to everyone's unspoken question, Dylan Stoddard is with me on the platform because, as of today, he will be assisting me in the responsibility and privilege of pastoring this congregation." Spontaneous applause answered him. "Dylan has agreed to take this job on a volunteer basis, while we evaluate the need for and feasibility of a full-time paid assistant pastor. He's taken a job at the sawmill to support himself in the meantime. For those of you who may not be aware, Dylan is in a time of transition in another area of his life. He and Leslie Carlson are engaged to be married as soon as she finishes her studies through our Bible school. The Carlsons have been part of our church family since before Leslie was born, so she's well familiar with the joys of church life. Leslie, would you please stand?"

Feeling like a bug under a microscope, she did as he asked. The round of applause made her feel both evaluated and welcomed. She took her seat again quickly.

"With that taken care of, let's stand and open with Hymn 152, 'Crown Him with Many Crowns.'"

The hymn had long been one of Leslie's favorites. A majestic melody and thought-provoking words combined to create an expression of worship from her heart. By the time the choir finished their musical presentation, which always immediately preceded the sermon, her earlier emotional turmoil had settled into a comforting sense of peace. Pastor Jim moved to the pulpit again. "This morning seems as good a time as any for Dylan to tell us the story of his walk with God so far. Please listen carefully to the first of what I'm sure will be many messages we'll hear from him. We're glad to have you with us, Dylan." He turned to shake hands with his new assistant.

Leslie felt like an icy wind had just whipped her breath away. Her stomach couldn't have felt any tighter had she been the one behind the pulpit. Yet his face showed only his joy at doing something for which he'd prepared for several years. Though she'd heard the details before, this time Leslie realized how God had arranged those details to make him the man he'd become. He told of growing up in a Christian home that had seemed perfect until his only sister developed anorexia nervosa. Without embarrassment, he also described the feelings which prompted him to leave his family without warning for a job on an oil rig, and then how the influence of a member of Heritage Christian Assembly, Ken Smith, enticed Dylan back into fellowship with God, which then helped him mend his relationship with his family. An unusual hush gripped the congregation as he spoke, indicating others besides Leslie felt the Presence that flowed through his words. For those twenty minutes, the man she loved had become a divine instrument. When he sat down, Pastor Jim didn't hurry back to the pulpit. He looked to the pianist, who began softly playing "How Great Thou Art." The service didn't end in a formal way. Gradually, and quietly, people just drifted out of the sanctuary while the instrumental worship continued. Leslie waited in her seat until Dylan left the platform. As soon as she looked into his eyes, she knew she didn't need to say a word. His spirit had been touched as had his listeners', and like them, he'd been awed.

eight

Leslie stood between Dylan and Theresa in a receiving line just outside the sanctuary door in an area referred to as the fellowship hall. The ladies of the congregation had planned this reception for the Sunday of Dylan's introduction to welcome him and Leslie in their new roles, but their plans had dissolved unnoticed in the quiet, contemplative spirit that followed Dylan's testimony. Now, a week later, coffee urns, teapots, and platters of sweet treats sat on tables on the other side of the room. Her hand felt numb from the number of times it had been squeezed by well-meaning folk unaware of the strength of their grip. Yet the warmth and welcome from these people with whom she'd had varying degrees of acquaintance since her childhood kept her smiling and gracious.

With delight, she noticed a short, wiry lady with white hair moving toward them in the line. "Look," she whispered to Dylan. "Granny Maxwell's back."

Granny emerged twinkling and breathless from Dylan's hug to bestow a similar embrace on Leslie. "Look at th' two o' ye. I'm so proud I could burst."

Leslie didn't know how to accept the praise. "I can hardly wait to hear all about your trip. Did you get to visit both your sons?"

"Absolutely," Granny confirmed with an enthusiastic nod. "Ye will ha' to come over soon and see me pictures."

"We'd love to," Leslie assured her.

Not all of the hand-shakers were so cordial. James barely

disguised his animosity with a smile. "So, Brother Stoddard, do you feel ready to live up to the high standards our church expects of its staff?"

Dylan said nothing, so James moved on to greet Leslie. "If you ever need someone to talk to, I hope you won't hesitate to call on me."

She took a small step backward to turn his attempt at a hug into a handshake and mumbled "thank you," for lack of anything better to say. James moved on down the line, with charming comments for both Theresa and Pastor Jim. Leslie glanced at Dylan to find him watching her with barely concealed amusement. Quickly, they turned back to the continuing progression of well-wishers.

Later in the afternoon, slouched on beanbag chairs in the Carlson family room, they shared a hearty laugh at James's expense. "I shouldn't laugh at him," Dylan confessed, "but he's so absurd."

"On Friday, he told me he expected to do his pastoral internship as Heritage's assistant pastor," Leslie told him. "The last couple of weeks can't have been easy for him."

Dylan agreed. "His bottomless self-confidence must have trembled at least a little."

"But if he thinks I'm going to tell him my troubles, he's got to be demented." She laughed again, but he didn't join in.

"Leslie, please be careful of him." His gaze reflected deep concern.

"I'm not worried. He's just a self-absorbed windbag."

"Don't underestimate him, sweetheart. He thinks you made the wrong choice, falling in love with me, and he's going to try everything he knows to make you change your mind."

She looked at him incredulously. "While he's annoying,

I wouldn't consider him vicious. Besides, how is my love life any concern of his?"

"He fancies himself in love with you." Dylan's eyes twinkled mischievously. "I certainly can't blame him for that."

"But I never gave him any reason to think I cared about him. Where does he think he gets the right to pass judgment on my decisions?"

"The same place he gets the right to pass judgment on anyone and everyone he meets. Only in your case, he's more focused than usual."

The ringing telephone cut off her next indignant response. She leaned across him to answer the extension on a low table beside the couch. "Hello?"

"Hi. It's Karen. I just wanted to call and congratulate you and Dylan on his new job. Li'l Brad was fussy, so we weren't able to stay for the reception."

"How is my favorite nephew now?"

"Finally asleep for the afternoon. I wanted to get him down for his nap before I called you because my call might take a few minutes."

A tiny alarm bell sounded in Leslie's mind. "What's up?"

"Are you sure of what you're getting into?"

"You mean in marrying Dylan?" At her words, he gently lifted the phone onto the floor, then pulled her back to lean against his shoulder.

"Don't get me wrong," Karen hastily explained herself. "I think Dylan's a great guy. But are you sure you want to deal with the pressures of him being in the ministry while you're trying to finish your schooling? I know from experience how hard a long engagement can be, especially in your last year of school."

Leslie had learned long ago how to stay calm when her

older sister started giving advice. *Ask questions rather than respond defensively to the oddball statements,* she reminded herself. "What would you suggest?"

"I'd expect him to keep working at the rigs until you were married. You just don't need the extra stress."

"Why do you think this will be so stressful?"

"People are going to expect so much of you. You're not just Leslie Carlson anymore. You're the assistant pastor's soon-to-be-wife, and you'll have an image to maintain."

Leslie rejected the temptation to try to make Karen adopt a different point of view. "Maybe you should talk with Dad and Dylan about this. They're the ones who want me to finish my last year of school."

Karen laughed, a tittery sound that always irritated Leslie. "They wouldn't listen to me. Anyway, I need to get the laundry out of the dryer. Talk to you later."

Dylan replaced the telephone receiver. "Is your sister trying to improve your life again?"

Leslie nodded against his chest. "Too bad there isn't some way we can focus her and James on each other. We'd solve two problems simultaneously."

Yet in the following weeks, Leslie began to agree with those who thought her life needed improvement, though not for the reasons they stated. A rare conversation with Andrew gave her a feeling of optimism even while an underlying sense of alarm strengthened. She'd been in the kitchen preparing supper when he hoisted himself up on the counter. "What's cookin', sis?"

"Hamburger and macaroni casserole." She smiled in his direction, glad he appeared willing to talk. "How was your day?"

"Same old stuff." Snitching a carrot she'd just peeled for the salad, he crunched between words. "An hour of physio, a couple of hours at school, another hour of physio, two more hours of school, two hours of physio, and home. Pretty exciting stuff, eh?"

"Is your leg feeling any stronger?" Gently, she pushed both legs aside so she could retrieve the cheese grater from a cupboard beneath his perch.

"Some, I guess. I still can't walk very far on it, much less run." The gloom he'd carried so frequently of late crept into his voice again.

Leslie knew he feared more than anything being unable to make the basketball team. Any reassurance she could offer would be just hopeful speculation. "What about the rest of you? How do your innards feel?"

He grinned at her terminology. "As long as I eat lots of rabbit food and stay away from high fat stuff, I'm okay."

Testing his nutritional knowledge, she asked, "What constitutes high fat stuff?"

"Desserts, anything with a lot of butter or margarine, McDonalds. Actually, most of what you cook is fine. I never noticed before how much low-fat stuff you feed us all the time."

"I've tried to take good care of you guys. What happens when you eat the wrong food?"

"I just get majorly pukey." He laughed at her disapproving look. "What I meant to say is I become acutely nauseated. Better?"

"Much. So where did you learn all these nutritional details?"

"Just lookin' around. It's not hard to figure out when you know what you're lookin' for." He tossed a pinch of grated cheese into his mouth. "Low-fat mozzarella, a good source of protein."

His answer sparked a thousand more questions in her

mind, but she didn't want to sound like an interrogator. She grinned at him again. "I'm sorry. I didn't mean to turn this into a personal version of Twenty Questions."

"'Sokay." He pulled the scrunchie off her low ponytail. "At least you still care about me."

His statement stopped her short. Looking straight into his face, she asked, "Why wouldn't I?"

His gaze dropped to the floor. "Just 'cuz," he mumbled before dropping her scrunchie on the counter and vanishing out of the kitchen.

If Andrew's troubles weren't enough, Leslie found it increasingly difficult to ignore the feeling Dylan had abandoned her. She understood when he didn't have time to talk during the week because of his dual jobs. But weekends were little better. He rarely called on Saturdays except for short chats that only left her craving more of his attention. Sundays were even worse. For one thing, she felt like the entire congregation watched every move they made when together and heard every word. She made a point to be in Pastor Jim's study each Sunday for pre-service prayer since her family always arrived at church at least twenty minutes early. Even though he greeted her affectionately and held her hand throughout the prayer, she'd begun to wonder if he'd even notice her absence. Occasionally, she'd notice him watching her with the special look meant just for her, but then someone else would claim his attention and the expression would be gone.

A little over a month after Granny Maxwell's return from her trip, Leslie entered the sanctuary after prayer time to find her usual seat with her family occupied. Granny discreetly gestured toward the empty seat beside her, and Leslie slid gratefully into place. After the service, Granny said nothing while Leslie watched Dylan leave the platform while talking with Pastor Jim, greet a couple of teens, then leave the room with one of the deacons. Leslie rehearsed her mental pep-talk. *This is what it's going to be like when Dylan is senior pastor. If I can't handle not being the center of his attention at all times, I'll just make his ministry more difficult.*

Granny laid a gentle arm across Leslie's shoulders. "Ye haven't been ta visit me yet, luv."

Leslie heard the unspoken message. Her dear Scottish friend wouldn't pry, but she wanted to listen if Leslie felt like talking. What would have sounded reproving from someone else, from Granny represented two opportunities. She could answer the obvious question with an explanation of her schedule. Or she could accept the offered comfort and open her heart. "I've been hoping Dylan would have time to come with me." Hearing her own words made her eyes fill with unstoppable tears. Once her heartache found a bit of release, a flood of emotion swamped her. The harder she tried to stop, the worse the storm became.

Granny pulled Leslie into her arms, absorbing the younger woman's tears into her shoulder. In her comforting embrace, the weeping gradually eased.

At last, Leslie found herself able to look up. "I'm sorry. I didn't mean to fall apart on you."

"Ye needed ta let go somewhere." Granny studied her with lovingly perceptive blue eyes. "How aboot spendin' the afternoon wi' me? I'd enjoy the company."

Her offer sounded like a bit of heaven. Leslie knew she'd be pampered and wouldn't be expected to do a thing other than enjoy it. She embraced her older friend gratefully. "And I'd love to come, though I need to tell Dad."

Granny nodded. "I'll wait for ye by the front door."

Dad endorsed Leslie's plans heartily. "Good for you. You

need some pampering."

It only took a matter of minutes for the two women to cross the parking lot between the church and the seniors' complex. True to form, Granny directed Leslie toward one of the soft, deep chairs in her living room. "Have a seat, luv. 'Twill take me just a moment to scramble us up some lunch."

Leslie relaxed into the chair, resting her head against its soft, high back. This quiet, comforting place made it easy to let go of her problems. In less time than seemed possible, Granny returned with two plates stacked with homemade rolls, two kinds of cheese, and slices of cold meat, tomatoes, and dill pickles. "'Tisn't fancy, but should help us keep body and soul on speaking terms."

Leslie reached for one of the plates with a smile of gratitude. Granny briefly said grace over the meal, then settled back against the couch. "So tell me what's been happenin' since I left. I notice ye've acquired a lovely ring."

Just looking at the gemstones brought warm reassurance, along with a smile. "He gave it to me about a month ago, the same night he told me about Pastor Jim's job offer." She described the dinner at Papa Joe's and the effort her fiancé had put into making the evening memorable.

"How long did it take him ta make up his mind aboot the church?" Granny set her plate in her lap, as if Leslie's answer were of great importance.

Leslie chuckled, remembering. "Close to a month, actually. He was really uncertain about what effect his job might have on me."

"He's a good man, that one." Granny nodded approvingly. "And what aboot the rest of your family?"

"Some things never change." Leslie sighed heavily. She began slowly, trying to remember the important details of her family's life since Andrew's release from the hospital in July. Finally, she concluded, "Vince is still angry with Andrew, and I have a hunch Andrew's struggling harder with alcoholism than he's letting any of us see."

Granny didn't respond right away. She reached for Leslie's empty plate, which she set on top of her own. "Are ye still hungry?"

"No, thanks. The sandwich was delicious."

Granny carried the dishes to the kitchen and returned with a tea pot under a cozy and two china cups on saucers. "This is a special blend of tea I picked up in Nova Scotia at Rita's Tea Room."

"Really?!" Leslie breathed the aroma from her steaming cup. "I've wanted to visit there for the longest time. Rita MacNeil is one of my favorite Canadian singers. Did you get to see her in person?"

Granny grinned with delight. "Yes, I did. She's just as approachable and gentle as she seems in concert. My boys remembered how much I enjoy her music, so they made sure they took me to the Tea Room on an evening when she'd be there. She even let my grandson take a picture of her and me together."

"That's wonderful! I'd like a copy, if you don't mind." Leslie sipped her hot drink. "This tea is really nice, too."

Granny smiled mysteriously and disappeared into her room for a couple of moments. She returned with a gift-wrapped package. "I brought this back for you."

Leslie set her cup and saucer on the coffee table before accepting the package and Granny's accompanying hug. Tears struggled at the edges of her eyes. "I don't know what to say. "It's so sweet of you to have thought of me." She pulled the ribbon and wrapping paper away, then opened the box. A package of tea nestled inside a china mug, both bearing a picture of the Tea Room. A cassette tape snuggled against the cup. She lifted it from the box, reading with delight, "Rita MacNeil—The Collection." A stiff piece of paper fell to the floor. Picking it up, she realized it was the photograph she'd requested.

"As soon as Rita agreed to stand with me for the picture, I knew you'd want a copy," Granny explained. "Since you enjoy her music so much, I thought the other bits would make you a nice gift, as well."

"Nice bits," Leslie repeated disbelievingly. The cup felt delicate, valuable because of its very fragility. "I'm still overwhelmed you bought these with me in mind. They're treasures."

"I'm glad ye like them, luv. 'Twas my joy to bring them for you." She studied Leslie in the pause before she spoke again. "I don't have any insights for your heartaches, child. All I can say is I know you'll find your way through this just like you have everything that's come before. You're a strong woman."

"Right now I don't feel very strong." The words came out in a whisper.

Granny wrapped her arms around Leslie. "Feelin's don't matter a bit. You're strong because you know you're loved—by me, by your family, by your God, and especially by your over-busy young man."

nine

A new week began without any further contact between Leslie and Dylan. She had no idea what activities occupied his time; she only knew a loneliness deeper than anything she'd felt before. At times she even wondered if this might be the beginning of the end of their dreams. Her home-related frustrations lost their significance. Her emotional resources now focused solely on the love she treasured but felt slipping out of reach.

On Thursday just before lunch, she passed through the student lounge to pick up a sandwich on her way to the administration building, where she'd spend the afternoon constructing a bookkeeping spreadsheet for her latest university assignment. Theresa and Granny Maxwell greeted her from a table near the door.

"Do you have time for lunch?" Theresa asked.

Leslie shrugged. "I was just going to eat a sandwich while I worked."

A look passed between the two women, then Granny stood decisively. "Then we're takin' ye away, luv. Ye look in desp'rit need of a break."

Leslie dredged up her warmest smile for the two ladies. "Where are you taking me?"

"Somewhere quiet and relaxing," Theresa responded, tucking her arm around Leslie's. "Do you have to be back at any specific time?"

"Not really." Leslie shrugged again. "As long as I get my assignments in on time, no one seems concerned with when I actually do the work."

The cafe they took her to occupied a small house in downtown Nipson. Walls between the main rooms had been partially taken out to create more dining space, yet small alcoves still existed that made ideal nooks for private conversations. Granny requested one of the secluded tables. Leslie didn't feel hungry for anything particular, so Theresa ordered for the three of them. "Corn chowder to start," she told the waitress, "then hot ham and cheese sandwiches. We'll talk about dessert later." As soon as the waitress scurried off, Theresa turned toward Leslie. "You're having a rough time."

Though a statement rather than a question, the words communicated a wealth of caring and nearly dissolved Leslie's composure. She nodded. Granny clasped one of her hands.

Theresa studied her placemat, then looked back at Leslie with years of memories in her eyes. "I've wished many times there were a way to prepare young women for what pastoral work does to the men they love. Except for a very few possible exceptions, every pastor's wife has felt just like what I've seen in your eyes the past couple of weeks. I don't pretend to know exactly how you're feeling, but I recognize a couple of symptoms. How much time have you and Dylan spent together since his first Sunday?"

Leslie had mentally rehearsed the occasions so often, she didn't need to ponder her answer. "Two Sunday afternoons." For fear they'd think ill of Dylan, she added, "Between his job at the mill and working at the church, he doesn't have much time."

"Nothing would be different if he were only at the church." Theresa made the statement without criticism. "Somehow church work gives those involved the feeling they aren't giving enough unless they're giving everything. I don't know whether it's the expectations people put on their pastors or the pastors' genuine desire to serve God and his people as best they know how. Whatever the cause, those of us who love these men end up hurting and feeling guilty at the same time. I remember asking God why He hadn't told Jim to stay unmarried if He wanted him to be a pastor. I felt like I had to compete with God for Jim's attention."

She paused while the waitress placed steaming bowls of chowder in front of them. The three women bowed their heads while Granny prayed aloud. "Our Feyther, we thank Thee for our food and for the opportunity to encourage our friend. We ask for Your wisdom and comfort for her as we visit together and for Your healing of the breach which has grown between her and Dylan as they've sought to serve You. Thank You for Your love. Amen."

Leslie had to blink back ever-present tears before she could begin eating. A glimmer of hope eased a bit of her heartache. When she could trust her voice not to wobble, she asked Theresa, "Is this what you and Pastor Jim were talking about when you said you almost lost your marriage?"

Theresa nodded. "In part. Our struggle had gone on much longer, though. If any of the older folk in our congregation noticed our trouble, they were too intimidated by our position to say anything."

"What happened?"

The waitress took away their soup bowls and replaced them with plates holding tender fresh vegetable sticks and hot sandwiches.

"We'd been married a little over four years. Jim came home from a deacon's meeting one night to find me in tears.

He immediately asked what was wrong, but I couldn't tell him. When I tried to talk, only sobs would come out. I cried myself to sleep on the living room couch with him sitting on the floor beside me. While I slept, he prayed. He could tell this part better than I can, but he says he didn't sleep at all that night. He asked God repeatedly to tell him what was wrong with me. The only answer he received was the verse from Ephesians which says husbands are to cherish their wives as their own bodies, and to give themselves as Christ gave Himself for the church."

"For the next two weeks, anytime either of us tried to talk, I'd start crying again. So rather than telling me in words how much he cared, he looked for ways to act out his love. I cooked and cleaned like a maniac just to give myself something to do. He learned how to help by watching what I did. On the rare occasions I relaxed with a book, he'd gently take the book from me and read aloud. We took long walks together, appreciating the outdoors and learning again to enjoy each other's company without exchanging a word."

"Then one night while I sat on the couch staring out the window, he knelt on the floor in front of me. He told me how he'd finally recognized what God had been trying to tell him. Christ had already given Himself for the church. He only needed Jim to serve the church. He intended Jim's selfless giving to be for me. With tears of his own, Jim asked my forgiveness for allowing the church to take my place in his attention."

Theresa had to stop and wipe her eyes as she remembered. Granny had to employ a hanky, too. Yet while Leslie felt the emotion of the story, she also felt like she hadn't yet heard what would make a difference for her. Thankfully, Theresa continued. "We sat up until the small hours talking, finally able to communicate honestly with each other. It felt as though Jim's undivided attention during those two weeks had healed the part of me that had kept silent for so long. As we talked, I realized the fault had been as much mine as his. I'd made a martyr of myself for the ministry. If I hadn't supported Jim's actions with my silence, we might not have had to come to a crisis."

As if on cue, the waitress appear to clear away the plates. "Dessert for anyone?" she inquired brightly, her tone contrasting uncomfortably with the intensity of emotion among the three women.

"Do you have banana cream pie?" Granny asked.

"Our cook made some just this morning, and we have fresh whipped cream for topping."

"Then we'll take two slices to share."

Leslie grinned. "You remembered the one dessert I can't resist."

Granny winked. "I may be old, but I'm not senile."

The pie tasted almost as good as Granny's homemade version. After several bites, Leslie found words for her feelings. "Dylan's under so much stress trying to juggle church and work. I'm afraid of putting one more demand on his time than he can handle."

"Has that boy ever told ye you're demandin' too much?" Granny asked sharply.

"No, but I'm afraid I might."

"Are ye sayin' ye don't trust him?" Granny's gaze bored into Leslie's heart. "Girl, that boy's love for ye is bigger than he is. His hurt would be bigger yet if he knew ye were afraid to talk to him."

Leslie swallowed the lump in her throat. "How do I get time alone with him? He works during the week and he's always busy on weekends."

Theresa smiled encouragingly. "If you're determined enough, something will work out. How about if you start by having dinner with us Sunday afternoon? I'll ask Jim to invite Dylan. Maybe while you're doing dishes you can ask him to set aside some time for the two of you to talk."

Leslie nodded. "I'm willing to try."

On Sunday morning, Dylan greeted her at the church door with a kiss. "We can get away with this since James isn't here yet," he teased.

"Pooh! As if we're worried about him," she replied disdainfully.

He kept his arm around her shoulders on the way to Pastor Jim's office. "Did you know we're invited to Quillans' for lunch today?"

His question reminded her unnecessarily of how unfamiliar they'd become with the details of each other's lives. "Theresa invited me when we were having lunch together the other day."

He looked at her inquiringly, but only said, "I'll make sure I don't get waylaid after the service, if you'll promise not to leave the sanctuary without me." His grin almost disguised the question in his eyes.

She found it impossible to concentrate on the service. Various possibilities for presenting her case came to mind, but each seemed destined to end in confrontation. By the time Pastor Jim gave the benediction, she wanted to follow Dad out to the car and forget this afternoon's appointment entirely. She'd rather live with uncertainty than make him angry with her appeal for something different.

For once he came directly from the platform to her side. "Shall we sneak out the back door?"

"Shouldn't we wait for the Quillans?"

He winked. "We can wait in the driveway."

"Then let's go." His eagerness to have even a few moments alone with her before their hosts arrived relaxed her nervousness. They ran hand-in-hand down the back hallway like a couple of teenagers. He pulled her through the throng still milling around the fellowship hall as though afraid he wouldn't make it if he even slowed down. Just before they reached the door, she heard someone call her name. With a sinking feeling, she glanced back.

"Leslie." Theresa approached, looking uncharacteristically agitated. "Something has come up, so Jim and I are going to be late getting home. I put a roast in to bake before church, but if it doesn't come out of the oven shortly, it'll be ruined. Here's my key. Would you mind going on in and rescuing it for me?"

"Sure. Is there anything else you'd like me to do?" She relished the opportunity for action, rather than just waiting around.

"I don't think so. Just make yourselves at home, and we'll be there as soon as we can."

The ride to the parsonage passed in silence. Leslie's thoughts still tumbled around how to tell Dylan what concerned her most. He seemed equally reluctant to make small talk. He pulled into the driveway and she waited for him to open her door. Some women she knew found the gesture demeaning. She felt flattered by the touch of gallantry as she walked up the porch steps ahead of him. Theresa's key unlocked the door easily. Leslie tossed her coat aside and hurried to the kitchen. A large piece of paper sat propped against the back of the stove.

"Dear Leslie and Dylan," she read. "This afternoon alone is our gift to you. We've made plans to have dinner with friends a little way out of town and won't be back until just before the evening service. Enjoy dinner and each other's company. Jim and Theresa."

Strong arms came around her from behind. "It looks like my boss and his wife have been reading my mind," he said softly against her hair.

She twisted around to face him. "You mean you noticed?"

"Not being able to spend time with you has been like trying to walk on a broken leg." He cupped his hands around her face and stroked her cheekbones with his thumbs. "I didn't mean to make you cry."

She buried her head against his shoulder while hot tears carried her anxiety away. "I thought you were too busy to miss me."

"Never." He held her tightly, stroking her hair until she'd regained control. "I'm sorry you felt abandoned, sweetheart."

She sniffed and looked up into the green eyes she'd missed so painfully. "I don't now."

Without moving his gaze from her face, he pulled a large, white square of cloth from his pocket. "When I noticed my handkerchiefs staying clean for three days in a row, I knew something was amiss."

She mopped her eyes, leaving mascara streaks on his hanky, then blew her nose. "I'm taking this home to wash it so you'll have to come pick it up."

He grinned, though something dimmed the twinkles in his eyes. "Let's rescue the roast, and then I'd like to discuss this further while we eat."

They worked together as easily as they had the first day the met, when he'd helped her clean up after a family party. A sign on the refrigerator door read, "Salad fixins in here." When she opened the door, a banana cream pie sat on the shelf. She laughed, then explained the joke to Dylan. He chuckled, too, and planted a quick kiss on her lips. "I'm sure her pie has nothing on your oatmeal cake."

When the food had all been placed on the table, he held out a chair at the end for her and took a seat along the side to her right. He reached for her hand, then gave thanks for the meal. He didn't say anything until their plates were full.

"I've been feeling abandoned, too," he finally commented quietly, watching her expression carefully.

An awful apprehension twisted her stomach. How had she failed him?

"Please don't take off on a guilt trip, Leslie-love." As usual, he read her fear correctly. "Someone told me not long ago about engagement being a time when two people learn to work together. I think this is just another lesson."

His gentle tone and the affection in his eyes reassured her. "Why do you feel abandoned?"

The smile she loved thanked her for trying to understand. "Any time I'm not sleeping or at the mill, I'm at the church. It would make my day to see you there more often than Sunday services." When she nodded, he continued. "I teach a College and Careers Sunday school class before the morning service and youth meetings on Fridays, as well as participating in a Bible study on Wednesday evenings. I know a lot of your time is taken up with your studies, but if you could be there even one other time during the week I'd feel less alone."

"Would you be able to pick me up on Sunday mornings if I were to come to Sunday school?" She forked another couple of potatoes onto her plate.

He took the bowl from her and helped himself to the remainder of its contents. "I'd love to."

Another thought occurred to her. "I've been wanting to get back into the choir now that my family's a bit back to normal. Aren't practices the hour before Bible study?"

He positively beamed. "So they are. I've been asked to take over as pianist for the Christmas cantata. The regular pianist doesn't think she'll have enough time to practice."

"Will you have the time?"

"I've missed being able to play the piano this summer almost as much as I missed you." His gaze met hers with an expression as tender as a kiss. "If I have to miss a few hours sleep to get my music back, it's well worth it. However, we digress. I've told you how I'd like you to change your schedule for me. How would you like me to change for you?"

His consideration engulfed her in a wave of tenderness. "Could you set aside either Saturday afternoons and evenings or Sunday afternoons for me? I'd like to have you all to myself for at least a couple hours every week."

"How about both Saturdays and Sundays?" He swallowed a final forkful of roast and enfolded her hand in his.

"Don't you need some of that time to plan your Sunday school lessons or a sermon?"

His grip on her hand tightened. "Not nearly as much as I need to be with you. If I'm desperate for preparation time, we'll work on the lesson together. I'd also be willing to consider offering you a ride to choir practice in exchange for supper with your family on Wednesday evenings."

She moved from her own chair into his lap and wrapped her arms around his neck. "I'll even promise oatmeal cake to seal the agreement."

ten

The Princess was waiting in the parking lot when Leslie left school Wednesday afternoon. In the amount of time it took her to recognize the car, its owner already had the passenger door open. "What a pleasant surprise," she greeted him.

His eyes twinkled merrily. "I wanted to make sure you followed through on your promise of dessert for tonight."

"I'm one step ahead of you, sir. I made it last night."

"What a woman!" he declared dramatically. Skillfully, he guided the vehicle into the late afternoon traffic that kept the main street beside the Bible school busy.

The rest of the family had agreed to an early supper so Leslie and Dylan wouldn't be late for the 6:30 choir practice. When the last crumbs of dessert had been eaten, Dad folded his napkin beside his plate with a loud sigh of contentment. "Dylan, would you believe my daughter hasn't made me dessert since the last time you were here? I've made up my mind. To ensure a regular supply of oatmeal cake, you hereby receive orders from your future father-in-law to appear at this table for supper at least once a week."

Because Dad and Mum shooed them out of the house as soon as they'd finished eating, Dylan and Leslie ended up at the church a full forty minutes before choir practice. Since he had a key, they unlocked the doors and went inside. Leslie had never been in the building before when it wasn't teeming with people. She followed him to a tiny room behind the pastor's office.

"My study," Dylan declared proudly. "Would you like to leave your jacket and purse here?"

She loved the light in his eyes that told her this room symbolized all he'd worked for and dreamed of since high school. Deliberately studying his height and broad shoulders, then peering back into the study, she asked, "Are you sure it's big enough?"

"It's just the right size," he assured her, tucking her purse into the bottom drawer of his desk. "If it were any bigger, there'd be enough room for my ego, too."

One of Theresa's remarks from several weeks ago returned to Leslie's memory. "They have a big faith, big hearts, big dreams." As she looked steadily into his eyes, she saw something new. His bigness had its roots in humility. Where she struggled with inferiority, he battled pride. The strength and confidence she admired lay only a whisper away from an overbearing ego. Her heart swelled with a love that must have shown in her eyes, because he gestured toward the door.

"I'd like to know what you're thinking, but something tells me this isn't a good place for it." His voice sounded strained, yet tender. "Hold that thought to tell me sometime when we're not alone." He led the way to the sanctuary, where he turned on only the lights above the piano. With the air of one greeting an old friend, he eased onto the piano bench and gently lifted the lid above the keys. Slowly, as if reacquainting himself with the motions, he ran chords and scales along the keyboard.

Leslie perched on the platform steps beside the piano. With her head propped in her hands and her elbows leaning on her knees, she closed her eyes. Had she been blindfolded and in a room with a hundred other pianists, she knew she could have recognized Dylan's playing. Even the notes from simple scales carried a message straight to her heart.

After only a short warm-up, he began playing worship music. Sometimes she recognized the tunes, other times she only sensed the musician's intent. For the first time in months, she felt an awareness of divine presence steal over her. Similar to the hush that had gripped the congregation the first morning Dylan preached, this time it seemed intended for her alone. She even lost the tingling consciousness of her love nearby. The comforting Presence wrapped itself around her, seeped into the irritated, hurting corners of her spirit, and bestowed peace. With it came the knowledge she could have drawn on this strength earlier if she'd only quieted herself and listened for its direction. Yet she felt no guilt for her failure, only a heartfelt determination not to separate herself again.

Music continuing flowing from the piano—first gentle, then jubilant, then restful again. She recognized the opening notes of her favorite piece, one of Dylan's compositions that made her think of Psalm 23. It began with lilting, joyful notes of trust. A run of high notes brought to mind a quiet stream, and a passage filled with minor chords depicted the valley. Full, glorious chords brought the selection to an end.

She opened her eyes to look at Dylan and to her surprise saw most of the choir seated on one side of the sanctuary. Most were still lost in the worship that had gripped her. Dylan became aware of them at almost the same time she did, and his playing gradually faded. The choir members slowly rose from their seats to make their way to the platform, looking as if they'd been roused from a restful afternoon nap. Pastor Jim slipped out the rear door of the sanctuary toward his office.

Being back in the choir felt better than wonderful. Almost everyone in the group had some musical experience, so their director, Steve Gray, didn't have to spend much time going over individual parts. Leslie relished being part of the many-voiced harmony. While they practiced numbers for Sunday services, Dylan stood behind her, blending his deep bass into the songs. About halfway through the practice, Steve handed out brightly colored cantata books and Dylan moved to the piano.

"We'll start on the opening number for tonight," Steve directed. "However, by next week, Dylan's going to be ready to play the music through for us. I think this is going to be a powerful presentation and not too difficult to learn."

Leslie also enjoyed the Bible study after choir practice. Pastor Jim opened the meeting with a few comments on the passage he'd selected, the thirteenth chapter of the Gospel of John. People volunteered their own ideas and a lively discussion ensued. After about ten minutes, Dylan pulled a piece of paper from the tablet he carried in the back of his Bible and began writing furiously. When she asked him about it later, he just grinned. "Come to Sunday school and you'll find out."

As promised, he picked her up early Sunday morning. She hung her jacket on the coat tree in one corner of his study, but carried her purse and Bible as she followed him to the upstairs room where the College and Careers class met. A coffee urn burbled on a table against the back wall. A teapot, swathed in a thick tea cozy, sat on the same table beside a huge box of doughnuts. Leslie recognized several Bible school students among the young people who milled around chatting, Styrofoam cups in hand. Dylan casually greeted each one by name on his way back to the refreshment table. By the time he'd poured a cup of coffee for himself and a cup of tea for Leslie, everyone had taken a seat. She wondered if she were imagining an air of anticipation.

"Let's take a look at John's Gospel, chapter thirteen," he began. Rather than standing in front of the class, he perched on top of the desk at the front of the room, one leg braced on the floor, the other dangling casually. "Verse three reads, 'Jesus knew that the Father had put all things under His power, and that He had come from God and was returning to God;' verses four and five, 'so He got up from the meal, took off His outer clothing and wrapped a towel around His waist. After that, He poured water into a basin and began to wash His disciples' feet, drying them with the towel that was wrapped around Him.'"

Dylan took a sip of coffee and continued. "During Wednesday night Bible study, I saw something in these verses I'd never seen before. Verse three is connected to verses four and five by the little word 'so.' In other words, because He knew His power, because He knew where He had come from and He knew where He was going, He was willing to perform one of the most menial tasks known to Jewish society. He was secure in His relationship with His Father, which enabled Him to be unconcerned about His reputation or dignity. What do you think?"

Ideas came slowly at first, then with gathering intensity as one comment sparked another. The lesson took on a life of its own.

"This makes me think of Jesus' response to the rich young ruler," one of the young women said. "He said that the law was wrapped up in two commandments—love the Lord with all you are, and love your neighbor as yourself."

"That's good!" encouraged a young man across the circle from her. "I'd never thought of these two statements of

Jesus' in connection with each other. But in both cases He seems to be saying if our relationship with God is secure, we'll be more concerned with meeting other people's needs than with our own reputations."

"It's the way Jesus Himself lived," another student pointed out. "He was always getting in trouble with the religious leaders for associating with people they felt were too sinful to be loved. They even accused him of being from Satan rather than from God because he shared meals with tax collectors and prostitutes."

Leslie looked from the class to its teacher. The expression on his face could only be described as glee. She realized this had been his goal in teaching this class—to see those who participated interpret Scripture for themselves. He wasn't here to force his doctrine into their minds, but rather to encourage them to know God for themselves.

A voice from the back of the room silenced conversation. "I think we're getting away from one of the most important elements of Christian living." Once he realized he had everyone's attention, James stood. "Our testimony before others is sometimes the only way they'll know what we believe. To borrow a phrase I've heard repeatedly this morning, we can share love unreservedly, but if the way we live doesn't reflect Christian standards people aren't going to be reached with the gospel."

For a couple of moments, Leslie thought James' remark had squelched further discussion. Dylan didn't look concerned, however. He simply waited to see what would happen next.

Finally, one of the quieter participants spoke up. Leslie recognized him as the fellow who'd accidentally run into her the first day of school. "James has a valid point. But I see it this way. We've already established that our actions toward other people are just an outgrowth of our relationship with God. Accordingly, our testimony would already be what it should because it's impossible to love God and yet live in a way which dishonors Him."

From there, the exchange of ideas flourished again. Eventually, Dylan broke in. "In the last few minutes of class, I'd like us to consider a practical application of what we've been discussing. Let me tell you a story.

"As you know, I work graveyard shift at the sawmill. I've become acquainted with a man about my age, Ray, who works the same shift. He is not only married and the father of four children, but he also supports his parents and his wife's parents, as well as any brothers and sisters who aren't able to find work. You see, he lives at Cairn Creek, which some of you may not know is a native community roughly 60 miles northwest of Nipson. It came into being about thirty years ago because half a dozen families decided they wanted to be free of the government welfare system, including the reservation and all its privileges and problems. They're trying their best to make it on their own without reference to their skin color or heritage. Unfortunately, one of Nipson's biggest problems is prejudice. How many native people have you seen here at Heritage?" He paused to let them consider the question.

"Because some of the natives in our area do take advantage of the welfare system and spend all their money at the bars and live on the streets, our community has labeled all natives lazy and irresponsible. A few of the Cairn Lake people have been able to find jobs, but not many. As a result, their living conditions are less than basic. Last weekend, Ray took me out for a visit. They live in shacks which desperately need work before winter. In several homes, windows have been broken and not repaired because there's no money. Most of the roofs leak, and a couple have holes through which you can see daylight. Some of the people have gone back on welfare out of desperation. Though the community is officially dry, alcoholism is a growing problem, especially among the younger people who see no hope for their lives being any better. There's a wide open opportunity for us to put this morning's lesson into practice, if we're willing to make the effort. How many would be willing to spend a day at Cairn Creek as part of a volunteer construction crew?" A number of hands went up immediately, as the buzzer signaled the end of the Sunday school period. Dylan laid a sheet of lined paper on the desk beside him. "I'm going to leave this sheet here for the next couple of weeks. Please don't sign up today, but rather think and pray about what you've heard. If you're still sure this is something God wants you to do, you can sign your name to the list next week. Class dismissed."

Leslie lingered in her seat while Dylan mingled with the group, shaking hands, giving encouragement, making each of the class members feel noticed and welcomed. "So what did you think?" He asked softly from behind her after the room had emptied, putting his hands on her shoulders.

"I've never experienced anything like it." She didn't know how to state her reaction any better.

"They're a good group, aren't they? All I have to do is throw an idea out and they take it from there. It makes leading the class almost easy."

She stood and turned to look into his face. "They are a good group, but they also have an exceptional teacher." An affectionately indulgent grin started in his eyes, but she put up her hand in a restraining gesture. "I'm not saying this out of any personal admiration for you. Dylan, you have a gift for whetting people's desire to know God personally. You made me, and made the other people in this class today, want to move as far away from routine Christianity as possible. Loving God is a reality for you and you make others want to experience the same reality."

To her surprise, tears gathered in the green eyes she loved. "It means a lot to hear you say so," he said huskily. "I only speak from my heart, and I feel honored He communicates through it."

She put her arms around him in a tight embrace, which he returned for several long moments. When he released her, he kept one arm around her shoulders while reaching for their Bibles on a chair beside them. "We'd better make tracks for Pastor Jim's office before he comes looking for us."

Later in the afternoon as the two of them relaxed in the family room, Leslie's thoughts returned to what she'd experienced both in Sunday school and on the Wednesday evening previously. "I'm glad you encouraged me to attend more church activities," she confided.

His gaze focused quickly on her. "Why so?"

"I wouldn't have wanted to miss seeing how God speaks to people through you. He's given you quite a gift."

He reached for her hand. "Something tells me I'm going to need you to help me remember these times." She looked at him questioningly. His eyes shone with love even while shadowed with whatever he anticipated for the future. "We're in the honeymoon stage at Heritage. They're pleased to have me there and I'm pleased to be there. Even though I don't have the experience Pastor Jim has, I know this will pass. I'll start seeing their humanity and they'll start seeing mine. We'll all have to work at remembering I'm there because I'm called, not because I'm popular."

She deposited a gentle kiss on his lips. "You'll always

be popular with me."

"How popular?" Teasing twinkles brightened his serious expression.

"Name your price."

He pretended to consider. "Another piece of cake."

"Ask and ye shall receive," Mum quoted, coming through the doorway with a small plate in each hand. "When Dan helped himself to more dessert, I guessed you might be wanting some, too."

"Now I know where your daughter gets her marvelous caring instincts." Dylan accepted his plate with a broad smile.

"She's had a good example," Dad informed them around a mouthful, following Mum with a plate in one hand and a fork in another. "Have you two settled the world's problems in here?"

Leslie chuckled. "Not even close."

Dad lowered himself into his easy chair. "I've been hearing good things about you from some of the men in church."

"That's nice to know," Dylan responded. "Leslie and I were just talking about a hunch I have about my honeymoon period at the church coming to an end."

"You're wise to recognize the probability. Unfortunately, since humans are the way they are, they don't seem able to stay content with anything for long."

Those thoughts lingered with Leslie through the ensuing weeks even while her studies, time with Dylan, church activities, and responsibilities with her family fell into a carefully managed rhythm. Though her schedule often felt filled to bursting, her hours with her fiancé made everything else bearable.

She told him so one Saturday evening in early October on their way to Pastor Jim and Theresa's for a church leadership Thanksgiving dinner. "Somehow the juggling act is worth it because it means I get to spend time with you on a regular basis."

"It's the same for me, Leslie-love." He glanced her way lovingly. "Having you participate with me in my church responsibilities encourages me more than I can put into words."

Leslie felt awkward attending this dinner. The deacons and their wives were there, as well as most of the men who had served with Dad during his years on the board. She couldn't shake the feeling of being a youngster in their eyes. Theresa greeted them at the door and whisked her off toward the kitchen. "I asked Dylan to bring you early so I'd have some help. I hope you don't mind."

"Of course not." She actually felt relieved to have something specific to do. "What do you need first?"

Theresa glanced around the obviously well-used kitchen. "I know this is a terrible thing to ask, but what I need most is to have dishes washed."

"I'll be happy to." Leslie pushed up the sleeves of her navy cotton sweater and accepted the apron Theresa offered to protect her long, full tan and navy skirt. "Do you host this dinner every year?"

"Yes. We started it in our first pastorate as a way of saying thanks to the men who support Jim in his pastoral responsibilities. The deacons can either lighten a pastor's load or make his job unbearable. We've experienced both, and the Heritage board has consistently had the helpful kind. They're not all easy to get along with, but they're one of the best groups we've worked with."

Leslie reviewed the couples in her mind while scrubbing pots. Ken Smith had long been a friend of Dad's, as well as a coworker of Dylan's at the rigs before a back injury put him into the hardware business. He and his wife,

Annette, had shared many meals with the Carlsons. Whe
Dad resigned from the board this spring, Ken had been th
one to read his letter to the congregation and his choked u
voice had told everyone how much he cared about Dad
Randy Butler had been selected by the congregation to fi
the deacon's position left open by Dad's resignation. He
and his wife, Kelli, were in their late twenties. Henry Dunn
had retired from law practice a couple of years earlier. Hi
wife, Joyce, owned an exclusive ladies clothing store i
downtown Nipson. Jan and Linda VanDyck owned one c
the largest beef ranches near Nipson.

She felt her knees get shaky when Henry Dunn's boom
ing voice at the front door announced his arrival. The ma
stood several inches taller than six feet and carried at leas
a hundred extra pounds on his large frame. His voice seeme
to come from the depths of his considerable belly, and h
had the demeanor of a man used to being heeded. Th
rumble of conversation from the living room grew loude
as couples continued arriving. Though she knew Dyla
had to stay and converse with the deacons, she still wishe
he could be beside her helping restore cleanliness to th
kitchen. After changing her wash water twice, she finall
wiped the last dish clean.

Theresa returned from putting food on the table as Lesli
pulled the plug for the last time. "You're finished already
I can't believe you tied into that mess so willingly. I jus
have the dressing and the cranberry sauce left to put on th
table and we can eat." She lowered her voice to a whispe
"Don't forget to take your apron off."

Leslie could picture Joyce Dunn's disapproving expres
sion if she left the apron on. The thought made her giggl
and Theresa's eyes twinkled in agreement.

When everyone had assembled, Jan VanDyck pronounce

a long, pompous blessing over the meal. Seated between Theresa and Dylan, Leslie felt under inspection, though no one singled her out for attention. Yet before the serving dishes had made it all the way around the table, she became aware of intense, though still subtle, scrutiny being directed at Dylan.

"I've heard some great reports on your Sunday school class, Dylan," Ken Smith commented. "My son, Kendall, hasn't shown this much interest in church since he was in grade school."

"There seems to be quite a Good Samaritan movement afoot among your youngsters," Henry pronounced. "Oh, for the idealism of youth."

"What do you mean?" Cathy Andersen asked, her round, smiling face reflecting genuine interest.

"I'm not sure who started it," Henry informed them, "but someone in the class has decided the Cairn Creek folk need help. They want to put together a volunteer crew to go out and winterize some of the homes out there."

Randy Butler set his fork down on his plate. "You mean the homes aren't winterized?"

"They're not really even homes," Dylan answered in a quiet tone Leslie recognized as a signal of intense self-control. "Most of them are little more than shacks about the size of this room and the living room put together, with as many as ten or twelve people living in one house."

"That's what they'd have you believe," Jan VanDyck said firmly. "They're not far from my ranch and some of them have come to me looking for work, they say. Ha! If I let one of them on my property, I'd find half my cattle gone the next morning."

Pastor Jim chuckled quickly before Dylan could retort. "This isn't the American West, Jan. Maybe they really do want honest work."

"Maybe so, maybe not." Jan nodded sagely. "I have enough reliable help with the guys already on my place."

"I've been out to Cairn Creek," Henry put in. "I'm not sure the time and materials it would take to fix those places up would be a good investment. I'm not saying it would be a waste, either."

Leslie heard the subtle message and knew Dylan did, too. She gently put a reassuring hand on his knee. He covered it with his own for a quick squeeze, acknowledging her support.

"How did you get interested in this project?" Gene Andersen asked Dylan, his quiet tones a welcome contrast to Henry's volume.

"I work the graveyard shift with Ray Esau, whose extended family makes up about half the community. He's one of the hardest working, most honest men on the crew."

"Is it true the community doesn't allow any drinking?" Annette Smith asked, starting the platter of turkey on a second trip around the table.

Dylan nodded. "They're officially a dry community, although the younger generation often defies the rules. The teenagers don't understand why their parents are willing to live in poverty rather than return to the welfare rolls."

"It sounds like the whole community could use some encouragement," Randy observed.

"As long as they don't interpret it as pity," Dylan said firmly. "Ray's told me how they feel about people who try to give them money. Food donations are seen as an insult to their ability to live off the land. They'll accept construction materials and help fixing up the houses, but only if they are included in the work crews. If we go once, I think we have to make a personal commitment to return at least once a month for social visits. We have to go as friends, not benefactors."

Jan ladled gravy onto the mountain of mashed potatoes in the middle of his plate. "What do the kids in your class think about all this?"

"I've asked the young adults to pray on it for a week before they commit themselves," Dylan responded with subtle emphasis.

"That's wise," Ken affirmed. "You can't do something like this on mere enthusiasm."

"Remember when the teens decided to shovel walks at the seniors' complex?" Linda VanDyck asked with a laugh. "That lasted about a month."

By the time Theresa served dessert, the conversation had shifted to lighter topics. All of the ladies worked together to wash dishes and clean the kitchen, and the evening ended on a pleasant note. Dylan and Leslie lingered after the others had left.

"What did you think about your first official function as Dylan's future wife?" Pastor Jim asked Leslie with a smile.

She didn't know how to put her observations into words without sounding critical. "It was educational."

He chuckled and looked at Dylan. "You handled yourself well tonight, son."

Dylan raised an eyebrow. "I have to admit I didn't expect opposition to Cairn Creek from this quarter."

"Don't let it shake you. The only perfect Man who's ever lived got crucified for it, so I doubt we'll find perfect men on any church board. Underneath their humanity are hearts who love God as best they know how. As long as you remember that, you won't be able to judge them too harshly and their judgments of you won't hurt as deeply."

eleven

The Carlson family dinner two days later proved much more relaxing. Since Thanksgiving Day in Canada fell on a Monday, Mum invited Dylan to spend Sunday night at the Carlson house. Everyone slept in late except Mum, who insisted on preparing dinner. "You and Dylan get little enough time together," she informed Leslie. "I'll take care of everything so you can just enjoy the day with him."

Leslie found the instructions harder to follow than she anticipated. Something kept propelling her toward the kitchen to see if she could help. However, Dylan or Dad always intercepted her with a distraction.

Brad and Karen arrived with Li'l Brad midafternoon. Andrew even emerged from his room for a few hours to join in games in the family room. Li'l Brad's toddler antics and Big Brad's loud jokes and booming laughter kept them all in high spirits. When Mum called everyone to dinner, Leslie looked around the gathering with a feeling of supreme contentment. Except for Vince's absence, this was her family at its loving best. They joined hands around the table while Dad asked the blessing. When everyone lifted their heads, Dylan pulled his and Leslie's still-joined hands below the tablecloth until the first of the serving dishes came by. Vince called while Mum was serving pie, so Leslie talked with him first. He sounded happy and glad to be in contact with them all. Everyone at the table except Andrew took a turn at the phone, including Li'l Brad.

When everyone had eaten more than enough, the men

took over cleanup while Mum and Karen bathed the toddler and put him into pajamas. Leslie occupied herself in
the living room with a novel, reveling in the laughter spill-
ing from the kitchen and smiling to herself when she heard
Andrew's chuckle.

Before Brad and Karen had to take their son home, Mum
called everyone to the table one last time. In the middle sat
cake decorated like a basketball. "Andrew's birthday is
day after tomorrow," she announced, "and I thought as
long as we're all together we should celebrate tonight. Son,
would you do the honors?" She extended the handle of a
knife toward Andrew, whose face struggled not to show
how pleased he felt. Brad struck up an off-key version of
"Happy Birthday."

"Aw, knock it off or I'll eat this whole thing myself,"
Andrew mumbled when the song ended. He gouged a huge
piece out of the cake and presented it to his brother-in-law,
then plopped a smaller piece on the tray of his nephew's
high chair. Obviously, being the focus of attention made
him uncomfortable, but Leslie could tell he was trying to
be pleasant. He continued handing out ragged slabs of cake
until everyone had been served.

Just before he plunged a fork into his own piece, Mum
set a decoratively-wrapped package in front of him. "Happy
Birthday, son."

Karen handed her plate to Brad, disappeared into the
entry way for a few moments, and reappeared with a smaller
gift. "Happy Birthday from us, too."

Andrew opened Brad and Karen's gift first, a pullover
sweater in shades of gray and blue. He held it against himself, smiling at them both. "Thanks, Karen. It's real nice."
Mum and Dad's present turned out to be a pair of high-
top, air-cushioned basketball shoes. Though he grinned with

delight, Leslie saw something like fear hovering in his eyes. He hugged both parents, then turned to her. "Did you forget something?"

"Since when have I ever forgotten your birthday?" Leslie retorted, glad to see his feistiness returning. "You know the tradition—you don't get my present until your actual birthday."

He slung his arm across her shoulder in an awkward half-hug. "I'm just buggin' ya'," he whispered.

She gave him a quick squeeze around the waist before he limped back to his chunk of cake, which he consumed in four huge bites. Picking up the shoes in one hand and the sweater in the other, he included everyone in a glance around the room. "Thanks, guys." He limped toward his bedroom, and Leslie heard the door click shut.

"How is he doing these days?" Brad asked in what was, for him, a quiet tone.

"Really well," Dad said. "His next appointment with the specialist is in three weeks and we're anticipating good news."

"Has he been having any other problems?" Karen never had been able to admit Andrew's addiction, as though it were too shameful a topic to be discussed aloud.

Dad's gaze met Leslie's briefly before he replied. "Between physio and school, he's been too busy to get into any trouble. He's turning out to be a typical Carlson teenager—just an all-round nice guy."

"Oh, Dad!" Karen giggled and lifted her son out of his high chair. "I think we'd better get this fellow home before he gets too tired to be a nice guy."

While Mum and Dad focused on the bustle typical of their grandson's departure, Leslie busied herself in the dining room, stacking plates, picking up wrapping paper, wiping the table and the high chair.

"May I help?" her favorite male voice inquired from above her as she stooped to pick up the cake fragments Li'l Brad had scattered.

She looked up with a smile. "Sure. You can wash cake plates if you like."

"I'll be happy to do that, too, but I actually meant help with whatever is making you worry."

"It's just Andrew," she admitted quietly, returning to a standing position. "I don't like to see him have to try so hard to be happy."

"I know." His green gaze studied her. When she didn't say anything further, he held out his arms. "Come here."

Dumping her handful of crumbs on the table, she moved into the haven of his embrace. He held her silently until she asked, "Do you think he'll start drinking again?"

"I don't know, Les'." His voice rumbled in his chest against her ear. "Any kind of addiction is hard to break. That's why they say an alcoholic will always be an alcoholic even if he's sober for fifty years."

"I just wish I could help him somehow."

He pushed her away only far enough to look into her eyes. "All you can do for him is reassure him of your love. He has to battle his cravings on his own."

The rest of the week progressed in a blur. Leslie's usual five-day studying schedule had to be compressed into four. Wednesday evening, she set her books aside for a time and knocked on Andrew's door.

His "come in" sounded less churlish than usual.

She held two packages toward him. "Happy Birthday, Andy."

His grin lit up her evening. "I'm glad you saved these until now."

"Why is that?"

He patted the bed beside where he'd been lying. "Go ahead and sit. I'm glad you didn't give these to me at the party because this is probably the last of my birthdays you'll still be at home." His observation told her how much it mattered to him.

"I'll probably still be in town. I'd even make you birthday dinner with Dylan and me if you want."

His brown eyes suddenly looked wiser than a teenager's. "Perhaps, but it still won't be the same. You'll have a different life."

"Does it bother you?"

"Kind of, but it's the way things should be. Dylan's a great guy and you're lucky to have found each other. I'm just going to miss you, that's all." Covering his unusual sentimentality, he ripped viciously at the tubular package. A large poster of Michael Jordan tipping a ball through a basketball hoop unfurled. Across the bottom, Leslie had written in black felt pen, "I believe in you." He stared at it without saying a word, then covered his eyes with one hand. When he looked at her, both eyes were red and wet. "Thanks, Leelee."

Not wanting to increase his discomfort, she gestured toward the other package. "You're not finished yet."

This time he unfurled a gray cotton sweatshirt with the Nike Air logo on it. "This is cool."

"I thought about writing on it, too, but I figured it would probably ruin the cool," she joked.

His gaze met hers directly. "I'll know what you meant every time I wear it."

Sunday morning, Dylan looked distressed when he picked her up for Sunday school. "Pastor Quillan called me about twenty minutes ago. Guess what happened at last night's deacons' meeting? They voted to put our Cairn Creek project on hold until I can present them with some quote 'practical' unquote fundraising ideas."

"Fundraising?" Leslie exclaimed in disbelief. "That will take months!"

"I know." Dylan sighed heavily. "We need to get the work done within the next month if it's going to happen before the weather gets really cold. I wonder if Henry Dunn would be so concerned about practicality if he were living in one of those shacks."

"Is he the one who made the decision?"

"It had to take a majority vote," Dylan conceded. "But you heard him and Jan VanDyck at the dinner last week. My guess is they persuaded Gene Andersen to vote with them because Ken Smith has offered to provide all the hammers, saws, and nails we can use, and Randy Butler approached me about going with us."

Quietness settled over Leslie like a warm blanket. She didn't say anything until they reached the parking lot and then words she didn't ponder beforehand came out of her mouth. "Our Heavenly Father gave you the idea for this project, Dylan, and nobody, not even Henry Dunn, can stand in His way. It looks like we'll just have to wait for a miracle."

Parking beside Pastor Jim's car at the side entrance of the church, Dylan stared blankly in front of them until she wondered if he'd heard her. At last he turned to face her, and she watched the hurt recede from his expression. "I guess I forgot Who's in charge. Thanks for the reminder, Leslie-love."

She maintained a continuous, silent prayer for him throughout Sunday school and the morning service. As soon as they arrived home, she hurried to the kitchen to stir up his favorite cake. She hadn't been planning dessert for to-day, but she needed to express her encouragement for him tangibly. He sat at the kitchen table watching, then smiling when he realized what she'd done.

He didn't say much during lunch. Afterward, he followed her to the family room as usual, but lay back on the couch rather than claiming his customary bean bag. Leslie dragged her bean bag to sit beside the couch. "Are you all right?"

He didn't open his eyes. "I started getting a headache during church this morning. I'll probably be okay after a nap."

She stroked the side of his face gently. "I guessed as much when you ate only a small piece of cake."

He acknowledged her teasing with a small smile and cap-tured her hand against his chest. In a matter of moments, his slow breathing told her he'd fallen asleep. He didn't stir when she slid her hand out of his grasp, or when she lifted his head to slip a pillow under it. She gently spread a blanket over him. Retrieving her half-finished novel from her bedroom, she leaned against the side of the couch to read and guard against anyone inadvertently waking him up.

Three hours later, she'd finished her book, and still he slept. Concerned, she brushed her hand across his fore-head, only to find it burning with fever. Her touch awak-ened him. He started to turn toward her with a smile, then groaned.

"What is it, Dylan?"

Without answering, he lurched off the couch and stumbled toward the door, letting the blanket fall. Awful retching sounds soon issued from the bathroom.

Leslie hurried to the kitchen for a pail, then to the up-stairs bathroom for some pain relieving tablets and a cool cloth. He'd collapsed back on the couch by the time she returned. She tenderly lay the cloth on his forehead and put the bucket within easy reach. Mum peered into the room, her forehead creased with concern. "Is Dylan sick?"

Leslie nodded. "I think he has the flu. Would you mind bringing a small glass of water?"

Mum came back quickly with the water and a package of crackers. "He'd better eat a couple of these before he tries taking any medication, or it will just come back up."

He nibbled the crackers without complaint. Leslie held the glass low beside his face so he could use the straw Mum had thoughtfully provided, rather than sitting up to drink. "I'm cold," he mumbled.

"It's the fever," Leslie assured him, spreading the blanket over him again.

He forced his eyes open. "I don't think I'll make it to church tonight. Would you call Pastor Jim?"

"Sure."

When Leslie started to get up, Mum put a gentle hand on her shoulder. "I'll do it."

The next time he awoke a couple of hours later, the two women persuaded him to move to the spare bedroom where he'd be more comfortable, and Dad loaned him a pair of pajamas. After another miserable trip to the bathroom, he collapsed in bed utterly exhausted. Leslie offered him a couple more crackers and a few sips of water, then pulled the covers up over him. When he didn't drift back to sleep immediately, she whispered, "Do you want me to stay or to leave you alone?"

He managed a feeble grin. "You're nice to have around." He dragged one arm out from under the covers and she wrapped her fingers around his hand. He returned her grip, but didn't let go. Pleased he hadn't asked her to leave, she sank to the floor beside him until sleep claimed him again.

She left the darkened room to rinse out his bucket and get more pain tablets for the next time he awoke. Dad met her in the hall. "I don't suppose you'll want to sleep upstairs tonight?"

"He says he likes having me there. I doubt I'll sleep much anyway."

Dad smiled sympathetically. "I didn't think so. How about if I make you a pallet on the floor? That way you can rest as long he doesn't need you."

Dylan grew worse during the night, as she suspected he would. He awoke at least every hour, so violently sick he had to use the bucket by his bed. He'd alternately thrash his covers off, then shudder with chills. She kept damp cloths handy, and fed him as much cool water as he'd drink. While he slept, she rinsed the bucket, replenished the water supply, and napped lightly. In the early hours of morning, his body finally calmed and he succumbed to a deep sleep. She could hear her parents moving around in the next room. Dad appeared in the doorway and whispered, "How's he doing?"

She moved to the hallway before speaking. "Better, I think. It was a rough night."

"You look like it." He smoothed her tangled hair back from her face. "He looks like he'll sleep for awhile. Why don't you catch some sleep yourself? Mum's up and can listen for him if he needs anything."

"Thanks." Her weariness didn't overwhelm her until she made it to her room. No longer burdened with concern for Dylan, her entire body collapsed as she lowered herself onto her bed. When she emerged from a drugging sleep, her bedside clock indicated ten minutes past two in the afternoon. Looking down at herself, she realized she hadn't changed out of her clothes or even crawled beneath her covers. A quick shower restored her alertness. She dressed in her favorite sweatsuit, a dark green tunic with tiny peach and yellow flowers matched with dark green stirrup pants. A pair of peach slouch socks matched the color in her top. Since her hair remained wet, she let it hang unconfined.

Dylan's eyes were open when she peered into his room. "Hi, soldier," she whispered.

He looked toward her with a faint grin. "Hi, yourself." His eyes looked glassy and his forehead still burned when she touched it.

"You're supposed to be getting better," she scolded gently.

"I'm trying." His eyes slid shut once more.

He obviously wouldn't be able to work tonight, so she found the phone number for the sawmill and informed the office. At bedtime, he didn't appear nearly as ill, so Leslie returned to her own room. By Tuesday morning, his fever had broken, though he remained weak. "I think I could handle a shower and shave if you wouldn't mind going to my apartment and getting my things," he requested when she looked in on him.

"I'd be glad to." She felt delighted to see the fever glaze gone from his face. Fishing his car keys out of his coat pocket, she hoped the Princess would start properly this morning. It didn't take long to drive to his apartment and find his shaving kit, toothbrush, and a fresh change of clothes. As she left the building, she noticed James jogging along the sidewalk across the street. She waved cheerily at him and drove back home. By the time she left for school, he'd managed a shower and was sleeping again.

Dylan didn't try going to work Tuesday evening and looked much stronger Wednesday morning. Leslie felt only faintly surprised to see him still at the house when she came home from school. "I didn't have the energy to drive home for the afternoon, then come back here for supper," he joked, "so your Mum let me pester her for the day."

"Pester, nothing," Mum objected. "I enjoyed your company."

Though choir practice went well, Leslie sensed something strange in the air during Bible study, almost as if she were the focus of negative attention. As she lingered in the fellowship hall while Dylan and Pastor Jim talked, conversations seemed to pause while she remained in hearing range, and she thought she heard her name mentioned at least twice.

By Sunday morning, there was no doubt. Somehow she and Dylan had become the subject of gossip. Pastor Jim revealed the problem during the prayer time in his study. "Someone has started a vicious rumor about the two of you living together. I haven't dignified it with a response yet, but I'd like to know if either of you have an idea how it got started."

The couple looked at each other in bewilderment. Profound hurt showed in Dylan's gaze as he said, "The only times we've been together have been here at church or at Dad and Mum Carlsons'."

Anger born out of Dylan's hurt boiled in Leslie. "Anyone who'd believe a thing like that is a fool! Whoever started it should be hung!"

"I'd be angry, too," Theresa soothed, "but letting it boil over isn't going to solve the problem."

"How is it a problem?" Leslie demanded. "Who honestly thinks the rumor is true?"

Regret lined Pastor Jim's face. "A couple of my deacons want a meeting with Dylan after this morning's service."

She couldn't believe her ears. "That's ridiculous."

Dylan lifted his head from his hands. "This is precisely what I feared the most when I took this job."

Leslie opened her mouth to argue, but Pastor Jim spoke first. "It's a rotten example of human behavior, but it's not outside our Heavenly Father's control. Let's leave it with Him so we can take part in the worship service with clean hearts." He bowed his head. "Our Lord and Father, we give to You this hurtful lie and its resulting confrontation this afternoon. We ask You to clear our hearts and minds for worship, and to turn this into something which brings glory to You. Help us to remember You faced lies and insults in Your ministry here and answered only with the love which took You to Calvary. Make us dispensers of that love, we ask, in Jesus' name, Amen."

Leslie took her place with the choir at the front of the congregation and tried not to feel like everyone watched her. Throughout the singing, she could hear Dylan's clear bass behind her, though not as strong as usual. Worship gradually pushed her trouble to the side.

The real struggle began when the choir filed down to their seats in the congregation just before the sermon. Now she had an unobstructed view of Dylan's face. Though he tried to conceal his turmoil, she could see how he suffered. His only comment in Pastor Jim's study had been, "This is what I feared most." This despicable situation hurt him so terribly because of its effect on her, she realized. If only she could help him see she felt only anger, not heartache.

Pastor Jim finally pronounced the benediction. Before Leslie had time to gather her Bible and purse, Granny stood beside her. "Would ye like to wait out this meetin' at me home? Mrs. Quillan will join us and the Pastor will call when it's over."

"Thank you." Leslie clung to Granny in a grateful hug.

A pair of strong arms came around them both from behind Leslie, and she recognized the smell of Dad's aftershave. When she turned to took at him, his expression communicated infinite love. "Hang in there, daughter," he said, drawing her into a hug all her own. "We'll be praying. Please let us know as soon as you hear anything."

Mum hugged her tightly as well, and Andrew laid a hand on her shoulder in an awkward gesture of sympathy. "I'll bet James started it," he whispered fiercely.

"We'll probably never know for sure," she responded, still too numbed with angry shock to think clearly.

But later in Granny's apartment after the three women had prayed together and Granny had brewed some tea, she found her thoughts clearing. Why did James's participation in this monstrous experience make so much sense? His gossiping nature aside, when had she and Dylan ever given him, or anyone else, reason to believe their relationship had become anything other than it should be? She curled more tightly into the chair and wrapped both hands around her tea mug, pondering. Then she remembered. Looking up, she saw Theresa watching her. "I think I've figured it out."

Theresa's eyebrows raised. "You mean a logical explanation exists?"

Leslie nodded. "When Dylan was sick last week, he stayed at our house. Wednesday morning before school, I went to his place to pick up fresh clothes and his shaving kit. As I was coming out, James Trindle jogged by on the other side of the street. I waved to him, thinking nothing of it. For some reason, he must have jumped to some pretty wild conclusions."

After a couple moments of stunned silence, both women

started chuckling. "If that isn't the silliest thing I ever heard." Granny shook her head. "If only people would mind themselves as intensely as they mind others."

"I'd better call Jim," Theresa announced. "Unless James is at the meeting, the men may not yet have figured it out." She dialed the phone number for the private line in the pastor's office. "How are things?" she inquired, then listened to what seemed like a long explanation. "Leslie just remembered it, too. That's why I was calling, just in case . . . Okay. . . We'll keep praying. Bye, love." She replaced the receiver and looked at Leslie. The concern in her eyes had intensified. "James was at the meeting. He, Henry, and Jan have left, but Jim, Ken, Randy, and Gene are still talking with Dylan. Your fiancé is taking this very hard."

"I know." Leslie leaned her head against the back of the chair. "He thinks he ought to be able to protect me. You heard him say this morning, he feared this kind of thing the most when he took on this church."

"But this could happen anywhere, not just in your home congregation," Granny exclaimed.

"I've tried telling him that, but he doesn't listen." Leslie sighed heavily. "Sometimes I think his incredible love for me is his biggest liability."

"Don't," Theresa retorted sharply. "Your love for each other is your greatest asset. It's easy to feel falsely responsible for the crazy problems you'll encounter in the ministry, but you can't give in to it. False guilt will separate you from the strength in each other. As long as you face the problems together, you'll both do fine."

twelve

In spite of all the encouragement Leslie, her parents, and Jim and Theresa could offer, Dylan remained locked behind a wall of hurt. Sparse attendance in Sunday school a week later didn't help, nor did the number of names crossed off the Cairn Creek volunteer list. Three weeks after the incident, only a handful of participants showed up for the Sunday morning class, James among them. Dylan's lesson felt like it came from a teacher's guide rather than from his heart. Leslie listened for his voice behind her in the choir, saddened to hear it muted. He did well at maintaining the appearance of an interested, caring assistant pastor, but she knew he'd lost the joy of his calling.

Finally, in the afternoon, she decided to try to get him to talk it out. Anything would be better than the sad effort to look as if nothing were wrong. "Would you talk to me, please?" she asked when they had settled onto the bean-bags in the family room.

His tired eyes brightened a little with affection. "Sure. About what?"

"About you." She laced her fingers through his.

His gaze shifted away from her face. "What about me?"

"You're hurting. I know it has something to do with what James did, but I don't understand why it's affected you so deeply. Can you try to explain it to me?"

He remained silent for so long, she thought he wouldn't answer. At last he said, "It's the lack of trust." She didn't reply, hoping he'd elaborate. "James's gossip-mongering hurt me because it reflected badly on you. But the reaction of the deacons is what I can't shake. Henry and Jan have made it clear they think of me as a kid to be tolerated until I get tired of this game and go on to something else."

"But you know Ken is your friend, and Randy obviously admires you a great deal."

"It's not the same, Les. Henry and Jan oppose every idea I have, simply because I thought of it. Working with them isn't ministry. It's politics."

"Have you talked with Pastor Jim about it?"

"All he can tell me is that this is the way pastoral work is sometimes. If so, I may have missed my calling."

Her stomach twisted painfully. If anyone were born to be a pastor, Dylan would be that person.

"Leslie," his voice dropped to a ragged whisper. "I'm to the point I'm not sure of anything anymore. All I know for certain is I want to follow whatever God's direction is for me, and I love you so much I can't bear the thought of being without you."

She wrapped her arms around his neck. "And I love you so much I'll make sure the thought doesn't linger."

Four days later, Leslie and Andrew left in the early morning for his second appointment with the Bayfield specialist. Mum had come down with the stomach flu the day before, so Dad chose to stay home with her, which left Leslie to do the driving. Andrew dozed for most of the trip, so she passed the miles praying for Dylan. They arrived in plenty of time for the late afternoon appointment.

After a forty-five minute exam, Dr. Wallace treated Andrew and Leslie to a rare smile. "You have a remarkable set of internal organs, my boy. In spite of all the abuse you've given them in the past year, you're looking healthier than a lot of people who come through my office. Just stay away from alcoholic beverages of any kind, and I shouldn't have to see you again."

A stormy look came over Andrew's face. "Why is everyone always after me about that? Don't they think I have any sense at all?"

Dr. Wallace removed his glasses and looked intently at Andrew. "Son, addictions have nothing to do with common sense. Those who've had the care of you realize what alcoholism has done to you emotionally as well as physically, even if you don't. Your glib dismissal of the problem in the past makes us wonder if you're aware of how serious your situation is." He paused, then spoke with deliberate emphasis. "You are addicted to alcohol, Andrew. If you give in to that addiction even once, it may just kill you."

Andrew's paleness told Leslie Dr. Wallace's words had registered. He stood and extended his hand. "I think I understand. Thank you, Doctor."

"That's what I'm here for." Dr. Wallace gave Andrew's hand a firm shake and clapped him on the shoulder. "I wish you the best."

Leslie had made arrangements for them to stay the night with Dylan's parents. The directions Mrs. Stoddard gave her over the phone brought them to the right house without mishap. Before she'd fully parked the car, both Stoddards came hurrying from the house to welcome them. Mrs. Stoddard hugged Leslie warmly, while Mr. Stoddard retrieved the overnight bags from the back seat.

"Did you have plans for this evening?" Mrs. Stoddard asked.

Leslie followed her up the walkway. "I brought some homework with me in case I had time for it, but other than that, nothing."

"Then how would you feel, Andrew, about going to a hockey game with our son, Steve? He managed to get tickets for the home team game tonight."

Andrew's eyes gleamed. "I'd like that."

"Good." Mrs. Stoddard took their coats and hung them in the closet just to the right of the large entry area that blended into a huge sunken living room. "Leslie, would you mind joining John and me for dinner? We'd like to treat you to our favorite restaurant."

"Sure, as long as I don't need any fancy clothes." She glanced down at the jeans and sweatshirt she'd traveled in all day.

"This place is as dressy or as casual as you choose. Your bedrooms are down here." Mrs. Stoddard led the way down four steps and through a family room. Three doors opened off one side, a bathroom flanked by two bedrooms. Mr. Stoddard placed one of the bags in each room, while his wife continued talking. "Feel free to lie down for a rest, take a shower, or whatever you'd like. Andrew, Steve should be home in about an hour and will want to leave almost right away. Leslie, we're in no rush for supper, so whenever you're ready to go is fine." Arm in arm, the gray-haired couple returned upstairs.

"What a posh place!" Andrew exclaimed in a stage whisper. "I didn't know Dylan's folks were so well off."

"Andy, that's not polite!" Leslie admonished, also in a whisper. "But you're right, this place is pretty nice."

The graciousness of their hosts enhanced the feeling of luxury. Leslie showered, changed into the outfit she'd brought for the next day—green denim pants with a green, rust, and brown plaid shirt—blow-dried her hair, and restored her makeup. By the time she finished, Andrew and Steve had already left.

"Steve's so excited about this game, he took off from work early. I think he and Andrew are going to enjoy themselves tonight," Mrs. Stoddard explained when Leslie joined her again.

"Andrew loves hockey almost as much as basketball," Leslie assured her. "Steve couldn't have thought of a nicer treat if he'd tried."

"Actually, it's a treat for Steve to have someone with whom to enjoy the game. John and I would rather watch it on TV than brave the crowds at the stadium. You look very nice. If you're ready, let's go get supper."

The meal lived up to Mrs. Stoddard's predictions. The food came well prepared, the waiter gave excellent service, and Leslie cherished the opportunity to become better acquainted with her future in-laws. Over dessert, the conversation finally turned to their common interest. "So how is our son doing?" Mr. Stoddard asked. "We haven't heard much from him lately."

Leslie briefly wondered how much to tell them, then decided to be transparently honest. "Not so well," she admitted. "He's feeling disillusioned with the ministry, and I suspect guilty for having doubts."

Mrs. Stoddard smiled. "That's my son, always expecting far more of himself than he would anyone else. Did anything particular precipitate the crisis?"

Leslie grinned wryly. "It's a rather detailed story, but I'll try to give you the highlights." By the time she finished a brief overview, both Dylan's parents were nodding with understanding.

"Sounds like a situation designed to make him dangerously introspective," Mr. Stoddard observed. "His troubles aside, how are you feeling about the situation?"

Leslie smiled, this time with genuine amusement. "I've

grown up in that church, and have known James since we were both in grade school. He can infuriate me sometimes, but he doesn't get under my skin the way he does Dylan's."

"Our son is an idealist, as well as being somewhat over-protective of those he loves." Mrs. Stoddard beckoned for the waiter to refill the large teapot in the center of the table. "James not only threatened your emotional well-being, he also forced Dylan to acknowledge once again how imperfect people can be."

"He's fixated on the two deacons who don't support him, rather than the two who do. The fifth one changes viewpoints with his socks."

Mr. Stoddard chuckled. "I think every church board has one of those. It sounds like Dylan's staying open with you, though."

"Only after I pushed," Leslie admitted. "What really scares me is his preoccupation with his ministry's effect on me. Originally, his concern was comforting. It's now become an obsession which is making him forget what he's called to do." She looked directly into Mrs. Stoddard's eyes, so similar to Dylan's. "I've never met anyone who can make God seem as knowable and fulfilling as Dylan does. He loves God with every part of his soul, and he makes others want to love that way, as well."

Mrs. Stoddard nodded agreement. "He's been that way since he was small. I remember passing his room one day when he was only about four years old. He seemed to be jabbering to himself, so I stopped to listen." Her eyes filled. "He was telling God how much he loved Him. God is as real to my son as the air he breathes."

"Why is he having such a hard time, then?"

When he spoke, Mr. Stoddard's voice carried the same gentle timbre Leslie had heard so often in his son's. "One of Dylan's weaknesses is his easy disillusionment with people who don't share his passion for God."

Leslie looked at him pleadingly. "Is there anything I can do to encourage him?"

"Just keep letting him know how much you love him." He slipped some money inside the folder with the bill presented by the waiter. "I hope you'll never hesitate to call us if you need bolstering while he struggles. Dylan's mom and I have talked at length about what a perfect match you are for our son. We're very grateful God brought you into his life."

Leslie had to blink back sudden tears. "It means a lot to hear you say so." The gathering of coats and purses and finding their way out to the car gave her emotions time to settle. Gradually, welcome serenity settled into Leslie's aching emotions.

Mr. Stoddard directed the car in silence, out of the parking lot, through two sets of stoplights and onto the freeway toward home. Finally his wife asked, "Has Dylan said anything to you about what he wants to do for Christmas?"

"Not yet." Leslie replied.

"When he does mention it, tell him we think he should stay in Nipson, provided both of you come visit us for New Year's."

Leslie took a moment to savor the feeling of being automatically considered part of Dylan's plans. "It sounds wonderful, and I'll mention it to him."

Weary from the mentally and emotionally draining day, she excused herself to bed soon after they arrived home. When she awoke feeling supremely rested, the clock beside her bed showed only 7:00 a.m. She dressed and tiptoed upstairs, wanting to let Andrew sleep until he chose to get up.

"Good morning," Mrs. Stoddard greeted her. "Would you like a full breakfast or just toast and tea?"

"Toast and tea sounds good." Leslie smiled her thanks. "My brother Vince hasn't left a message, has he?"

Mrs. Stoddard shook her head. "He knew you'd be here?"

"I left a message with student services Wednesday evening when we decided I'd be the one to bring Andrew down and after I'd talked with you. He must be having mid-terms or something." The explanation sounded plausible, but while she munched her toast she couldn't deny the hunch he'd just chosen not to call.

She and Andrew set out for home right after lunch. "Drive safely," Mr. Stoddard cautioned in a fatherly manner.

"And pass this along to Dylan." Mrs. Stoddard embraced Leslie again.

Leslie grinned. "With pleasure."

For the first hour of the trip, Andrew was enthused about the hockey game and asked about Leslie's evening. Then he lapsed into a pensive silence. She hoped he'd eventually confide in her if she left him alone. Yet by the time they reached Nipson around supper time, he'd still said little.

December arrived in a snowstorm that lasted three days. The wind and snow finally died down late Saturday afternoon. Dylan looked deeply worried when he arrived for dinner.

Leslie greeted him with a kiss. "What's the trouble?"

He shook his head. "I just can't get my mind off those folks at Cairn Creek. The wind will have whistled right through their homes, probably creating snow drifts in their kitchens. Why do people who have so much have to be so stingy?"

She responded only with a long hug, knowing words wouldn't ease his burden.

The next evening as the two of them entered the church for the evening service, Pastor Jim met them with a jubilant grin. "Come see what we found in this morning's offering." He beckoned toward his office.

As they entered the room, Leslie stepped to one side to allow Dylan an unhindered view of Pastor Jim's desk. Three offering envelopes without names or numbers, marked "Native Ministry," lay in a tidy row. Radiant joy broke across Dylan's face. "Isn't that something?" he breathed, then crushed Leslie in an ecstatic hug.

"There's over a thousand dollars there, so I'd suggest you assemble your work crew," Pastor Jim told them. "When God moves like this, even Henry Dunn can't argue with him."

Leslie laughed aloud, but Dylan didn't catch the humor. "Let's not mention Henry Dunn." Yet much of his sparkle had been restored by the miracle. When he talked to the small evening congregation about the project, those who heard felt his burden. He didn't ask for a show of hands, but concluded with, "Anyone who'd like to help, please meet me at the church at four o'clock Friday afternoon. Bring bedding and change of clothes so we can stay overnight and put in a full day Saturday."

When Dylan arrived to pick her up Friday afternoon, Andrew met them in the entry. "May I come?"

Dylan beamed. "Absolutely. We need as many men as we can get."

Leslie saw the flash of pleasure in her brother's eyes at the ready acceptance. Dylan let out a shout of laughter as soon as the church parking lot came into view. "Well, look at that!" At least a dozen cars had already arrived, and two more pulled in behind Dylan. By the time Ken Smith arrived with the supply truck loaded with lumber, shingles, windows, and tools, enough volunteers had shown up to fill the church bus. Jan VanDyck and Gene Andersen appeared just before Dylan loaded the last sleeping bag. "Do you have room for two more?" Jan called out in the deferential tone of a worker addressing his foreman.

"We always welcome more hands," Dylan responded jovially.

Pastor Jim approached. "How about if I head on out with the bus, and you and Leslie bring the supply truck?"

"Sure. Ray said we can unload at the community hall, and get organized from there."

"See you in about an hour, then."

Dylan whistled and hummed all the way to Cairn Creek. Leslie didn't try to interrupt him with conversation, delighted to see him so happy. The sight that greeted them at their destination, however, halted his singing. A village spread before them, comprised of buildings of varying shapes and sizes. Only a few looked habitable. Most appeared too small for a couple, much less an extended family. Their disrepair was every bit as bad as Dylan had described, and worse.

A man of medium height and friendly eyes came out of a long, low building that looked the best kept of all. He hopped up onto the running board of the truck as soon as Dylan braked to a stop. Dylan rolled down his window. "Leslie, this is Ray. Ray, my fiancée, Leslie."

Ray nodded to her, then looked back at Dylan. "Thanks for coming, man. Looks like you've got quite the crew assembled."

"I simply told them where I was going, and they asked to tag along. How would you suggest we get started?"

"You can unload your sleeping gear into the hall. Once everyone's inside, let's talk about what needs to be done.

I'll gather up my guys." He jumped down and jogged off toward one of the smaller houses.

Leslie wondered how well everyone would work together, but discovered she needn't have worried. Dylan split everyone up into groups of four, with a Cairn Creeker providing a fifth and directing the crew. As they watched the groups fan out across the village, carrying various supplies, he confided to Leslie, "Ray says if a community member has some direction in the way our work is carried out, they'll feel they've retained their pride. Let's go see what we can do for his house."

Darkness fell too soon after they arrived, but the villagers readily provided lanterns to light another two hours of work. When everyone returned to the hall, several ladies were there with baked fish and a fried bread called bannock. Even Jan accepted the meal graciously, sitting cross-legged on the floor with a plastic plate on one knee. They hadn't finished eating when a group of teenagers arrived with a collection of musical instruments. When one handed a guitar to Dylan, he passed it to Leslie. "This is the lady who can really play," he told the young fellow with a smile.

At first, the teens started out with a few popular songs. With his guitar, Ray subtly introduced a couple of heritage numbers from his own people. Then he led into the first verse of "The Old Rugged Cross" with a strong baritone. Leslie would have enjoyed hearing him sing solo, but the crowd joined in. The door to the hall opened repeatedly to admit more people. Hymn after hymn was requested, and the villagers seemed to know most of the words. Time lost relevance.

Despite a late bedtime, no one appeared reluctant when Dylan sounded a wake-up call. Two large restrooms at one end of the hall gave ample room for morning ablutions. Again the ladies appeared, this time bearing an unfamiliar yet tasty cereal. The group dispersed into the teams of the previous evening, and the ringing sounds of construction filled the morning air. No formal lunch break stopped the work. Instead, workers were plied with sandwiches of either bologna or peanut butter and honey. By dusk, the village looked like a new place.

The community hall was strangely deserted as workers trickled back to pack their bedding. Just before loading of the bus began, Ray stepped into the hall. "The people of Cairn Creek thank you," he said, his voice carrying easily in the tired, yet contented quiet. Your caring has shown us what real friendship can mean. In case you're wondering why no one's here to send you off, it's just the way of my people. They trust me to convey their gratitude to you and I do. You've not only given us help, but your acceptance of us has let us keep our dignity. You are welcome here any time, as friends." He backed out the door unceremoniously.

Dylan and Pastor Jim unloaded the remaining construction supplies from the truck, stacking them in the hall where they'd stay dry. Leslie helped the others stuff sleeping bags, pillows, and overnight cases into the luggage area of the bus. Tired volunteers claimed seats, with Ken Smith in the driver's position. Pastor Jim looked at Dylan with a glowing smile. "Isn't it amazing how God fulfills the dreams He gives us? I know it hasn't been easy for you to wait, but you can't argue with the results."

Dylan's smile looked strained. "Things have turned out well," he admitted.

Pastor Jim swung himself up into the bus, and with a couple short blasts of the horn, the vehicle lumbered back toward town. Dylan watched until it turned a corner out of sight. He moved toward the truck and opened the passenger door for Leslie. "Your carriage, ma'am."

Darkness obscured the snow-covered road. Since Dylan didn't appear eager for conversation, Leslie watched the night-shadowed trees along the side of the road, occasionally shifting her gaze to the constellations clearly visible above. They were about halfway home when she noticed with delight two glowing swaths across the sky. "Dylan," she whispered, "please stop."

He looked at her with concern. "What's wrong?"

"Nothing." She tugged at her door handle. "Look up there."

His affectionate chuckle reached her through the darkness. "The northern lights. I should have known." He joined her at the front of the truck, slipping between her and the vehicle. She reached back and pulled his arms around her.

They watched the lights increase in intensity, then begin to shimmer with color. She hooked her hands over his arms crossed in front of her. "Remember what you told me about the music of the lights being heard only in deep darkness?"

He murmured assent against her hair.

"I'm seeing something else up there tonight." She paused as the lights undulated in ballet-like movements, forming swirls and patches, then fanning out in swaths again. "It like they're not simply waiting for the darkness to disappear. They're dancing in it."

His arms tightened. "I hear you." The show overhead continued. Leslie wondered if she were imagining a sense of release in the strong form behind her. Then, in a ragged, low voice he began to talk. "I should be rejoicing tonight. The Cairn Creek people have been helped through a miracle by a larger group of volunteers than I ever envisioned. Yet the struggle it's taken still eats at me. While stubborn men dithered over practicality, Ray's family weathered a snow-storm in a building not even fit to be a summer shelter."

"Jan and Gene obviously had a change of heart," Leslie offered softly.

"Because it was easy, with a thousand dollars of specifi-cally designated money sitting there." His voice carried an unfamiliar tinge of bitterness. "The next time something like this comes up, they'll dance to Henry's tune just like they did when James stirred up trouble. They see me as a young upstart they have to control until I learn to be as staid as they are. I can't do it, Les. I won't." He leaned against her and his tone softened. "Maybe Henry's agenda is what I have to learn to dance through. In the past couple of weeks, I've seriously considered releasing you from our engagement and returning to the rigs."

A horrible numbing feeling washed over her as she turned to face him. "Re-re-release me?"

He pulled her against himself tightly. "Only because you shouldn't have to put up with my internal agonizing. Stand-ing here right now, I know I could never push you out of my life, regardless of how much I might want to for your own good. I need you too much, Les." His voice broke, and his head bowed against her shoulder.

The numb feeling receded, replaced by an assurance of the strength she could give him through her love. "Don't you dare try to get rid of me, Pastor Stoddard," she mur-mured against the front of his jacket. "I said I'd marry you and that's exactly what I intend to do."

He released his embrace to place his hands around her face and tip her head up to look at him. "I'm still not sure I'm going to stay with the church. Would you marry me even if I went back to the rigs?"

His words brought a stab of dismay, yet she looked

steadily into his eyes, hoping he could see the depth of her love. "I'm in love with a person, not a profession. I don't care what title you wear. Your heartache makes me hurt, too. If going back to the oil field is what you need, I'll love you all the way. Just make sure you get time off next summer for your wedding."

thirteen

As Christmas approached, Dylan's discouragement refused to lift. Occasionally the shadows in his eyes would brighten during a visit with Leslie and her family, but his face still showed signs of strain. Leslie sensed his involvement at church only continued because he didn't yet feel sure about leaving. Daily she prayed for the certainty of his calling to overcome his frustrations.

Andrew's outlook didn't improve either. Physiotherapy, basketball practice, and school kept him away from home. When he did have a rare evening with his family, his reluctance to talk bordered on sullenness. She tried to draw him out with questions about his game schedule, but he only answered with, "We don't know for sure yet."

Despite concern for the two men closest to her heart, her studies continued to flourish. She found her workload much less onerous than she'd anticipated, mostly because what she learned would be genuinely useful after graduation. Computer studies turned out to be particularly stimulating. In her practicum work in the school office, she found numerous ways computers would ease the workload of the full-time staff.

The office administrator, Marge Tyler, beamed with delight one Friday when Leslie showed her how to create form letters that could be merged with a file of student names and addresses for routine reminders. "Keep this up and I may have to offer you a full-time job next June," she warned.

"By that time, you'll be so organized you won't need me anymore," Leslie responded with a laugh, stacking homework into her book bag. "In the meantime, if I don't get myself out to the parking lot, I'll end up walking home."

"As if your dad would drive off without you," Mrs. Tyler scoffed.

Leslie just grinned. "See you next year."

Mrs. Tyler looked blank for a moment, then understanding dawned. "I'd forgotten Christmas break starts on Monday. Do you have any special plans for the holidays?"

"My brother's coming home from university, and Dylan and I will be going to visit his parents for few days. How about you?"

"All four of our children and their families will be with us this year. We'll have ten adults and fifteen children under the age of twelve for three days." She didn't look the slightest bit intimidated by the prospect.

"Have fun!" Leslie dashed out the door. At the car, Dad greeted her with a variation of his usual jibe. "Hey lady, either you or that bag has to stay. There's a legal load limit for this car, you know."

"Sure, sure," she responded. "Who's going to throw me out?"

Dad chuckled. "You win. Do you have anything special planned for tonight?"

"Just a course assignment due the first day after Christmas break. I figured if I got it done tonight, then I wouldn't have to worry about it during the holidays."

"You're doing well at keeping up with assignments, aren't you?"

"There's a lot of work to do, but it's not as difficult as I expected. I've even been able to keep my 3.8 grade average."

Dad raised his eyebrows in admiration. "That's no small feat. You've had a lot to carry emotionally at the same time."

She responded slowly. "I can't say I'm not worried about Dylan or Andrew, or even Vince, because I am. Somehow, though, I'm not burdened by the concern like I was in the spring when it was just Andrew."

"That's what the serenity prayer is all about." He slowed the car down to turn onto their street, then quoted, "'God, grant me the serenity to accept the things I cannot change, the courage to change the things I can, and the wisdom to know the difference.' If you can master it, you'll be well-equipped for a life in the ministry. Has Dylan said anything about his plans for Christmas?"

"Nothing. I'm not sure he's even aware of the season."

Dad didn't answer until he'd parked the car and they had reached the porch. "He's still pretty discouraged?"

She nodded. "You've stated it mildly."

He retrieved the day's mail from the mailbox, then held the front door open. "Maybe we should talk a bit after supper."

"I'd like that."

Her homework progressed smoothly. By supper time, only another hour of work remained. Mum placed a steaming bowl of chili and a basket of fresh buns on the table. "It smells delicious." Leslie gave her a gentle hug. "And thanks to you cooking tonight, I'm within a whisper of having no homework to do over the holidays."

But Dad's announcement at the end of the meal postponed her plans. "We're having family council in one hour." His conversational tone only reinforced the sense of purpose behind his words. Apprehension flashed in Andrew's eyes, and he left the table quickly; however, he appeared in the family room at the appointed hour. Mum brought in a large bowl of popcorn for everyone to share, and tall glasses of Pepsi for Andrew and Leslie. Dad followed with two cups of mocha, one of which he handed to Mum after she'd seated herself on the couch.

He settled into the easy chair he usually occupied at such meetings. Pulling an envelope from his shirt pocket, he looked at his family. "I received a letter from Dr. Wallace today. I thought we might have an easier time discussing its contents if we do so before Vince arrives tomorrow." He began to read from the two sheets of paper. "Dear Dr. and Mrs. Carlson. This letter is not within the scope of my duties as a consulting specialist, but rather an expression of concern from one parent to another.

"Your son, Andrew, is a fine young man in whom I've observed signs of exceptional talent both physically and intellectually. I am most impressed with his quick recovery from the circumstances which almost claimed his life six months ago.

"I fear, however, that his remarkable rehabilitation had led him to disregard how serious the consequences of his actions could have been or how easily he can undo what his body has accomplished so far.

"For many young people, the decision to include alcohol in their lives is merely risky. For Andrew, such a decision could be fatal. I'm aware he's not had a drink since his accident. His emotional state and attitude lead me to believe this has been due more to lack of opportunity than to a genuine decision on his part. With two teenaged sons of my own, I'm well aware the basketball season is now in full swing, and I'm sure he's already regained his position on the first string of his team. Each time his team celebrates a win, the temptation to join with his friends in an illegal victory beer will become stronger.

"Giving in to the temptation on one occasion may have no physiological effect. As I've stated before, however, it may have disastrous effect. Certainly, if he resumes frequent consumption of alcohol, his body's reaction will range from serious to deadly.

"I know your concern for your son is greater than mine. Perhaps what I've stated here will assist you guiding Andrew toward healthy choices and as long and happy a life as possible. Yours sincerely, Dr. P. D. Wallace."

Leslie watched Andrew throughout the reading. He'd settled his lanky frame into the corner of the couch, propped his feet on the cushions, and wrapped his arms around his knees. During the complimentary paragraphs, his face flushed with embarrassed gratification. Then he paled and his jaw tightened. Dad folded the pages back into his pocket. "Do you want to say anything, son?"

Andrew studied his knees for several moments, then muttered, "I've told him and you guys—"

Dad interrupted swiftly. "We're well aware of what you've told us. However, I've let your denial go on long enough. If nothing else, your attitude lately has been bearing an uncomfortable resemblance to the way you treated us almost a year ago when all this began. Whether you've started drinking again or not, we've sensed your vulnerability to the temptation. As a family, it's our responsibility to provide as much support as we can. The first step is getting rid of the denial."

"I'm not an alcoholic!" Andrew retorted in a rare display of temper.

Dad didn't raise his voice. "Would you please tell me your definition of an alcoholic?"

When Andrew didn't reply, Mum leaned toward him.

Her usually gentle voice softened even more as she asked, "Why are you afraid of admitting you are addicted to drinking?"

His defensiveness buckled. He looked at Leslie as though appealing to her to answer the question for him. She tried to communicate caring and support in her gaze, but remained silent. His face hardened again. "I haven't taken a single swallow of beer since I got hurt."

Dad gave him a penetrating look. "Are you telling us the truth?"

Andrew stared back at his knees, then looked up with false brightness. "Did I tell you guys I'm planning to enroll in Rocky Mountain Bible College after I graduate this year?"

For a moment, Leslie thought Dad would give up. He leaned against the back of his chair as if in resignation and closed his eyes. Then he opened them again. "I'm not sure you'll be accepted."

"Why not?" Andrew bristled with indignation.

"Because I'm on the admissions committee and I can recommend denial of your application."

His son's eyes filled with hurt. "Why would you do that? I told you I haven't taken a drink in over six months!"

Dad's smile communicated deep compassion as well as determination. "I'm not nearly as concerned about what you have or haven't swallowed as I am about your refusal to admit your weaknesses. I refuse to help you continue lying to yourself. Bible school is one of the easiest places in the world in which to hide from the person you really are. Unless you've learned to be honest with yourself before you arrive, you'll spend your time there simply learning how to be a better actor."

Andrew studied Dad's face, and his own expression softened. "You don't want me to be like Vince."

Leslie swallowed her gasp of surprise. Though Andrew had perceptively identified his brother's biggest problem, she wondered how Dad would respond.

With a small smile, he nodded. "I've tried never to use comparisons between the four of you to influence your behavior. In this case, however, you've shown commendable insight. You're right. I don't want you to turn into the kind of person Vince has become, not because I don't want you to be like him, but because I'd like to see you develop the real you. Dr. Wallace is right—you have an abundance of talent and potential. You'll never tap into it until you learn to be as perceptive about yourself as you are about others."

"What do you want me to do?" A touch of insolence almost covered the curiosity in his tone.

Dad ignored the insolence. "I'd like you to agree to fifty-two weekly sessions with a Christian counselor."

"You mean I have to spend a year with a shrink before I can start Bible school?" Dismay made his voice squawk.

"No." Dad shook his head. "Find yourself a counselor, even one of our local pastors, and sign an agreement with him for fifty-two sessions."

Andrew appeared to consider the possibilities, then asked, "Are we finished?"

"I think so." Dad snagged his arm as Andrew left the room in a hurry. "Son, please don't ever let yourself forget how much we love you."

Leslie wanted to follow her brother and enfold him in a comforting hug, but something inside restrained her. Dad had imposed the tough love Andrew needed. Any attempt on her part to soften the impact would hinder, if not neutralize, what might have been achieved.

"Do you want to talk about it?" Dad's gentle inquiry interrupted her contemplation.

She looked at him blankly. "Pardon me?"

"You look like you're thinking seriously about something. If you'd like to talk, we'd like to listen." He moved over to the couch, where he sat down close to Mum and placed an arm around her shoulders. She snuggled into his embrace.

Leslie grinned at the two of them. "You two are like a pair of teenagers."

Dad's eyebrows went up. "I recall you engaging in similar friendly behavior with a certain pastoral intern." When her smile died, he stopped teasing. Compassionate silence urged her to share her burden.

When she could speak around the lump in her throat, she asked, "Did you know he's considering going back to the oil patch?"

Dad nodded. "He stopped by the school last week to talk with me. He's worried about how his uncertainty is affecting you."

"And I'm worried about how it's affecting him, so I guess we're a matched pair." Though she wanted to pass the statement off as a joke, her laugh didn't sound convincing.

"Don't let his struggles make you doubt how well-matched you are," Dad advised. "As an illustration, do you have any doubts about his future as a pastor?"

"None." A surge of confidence dispelled her melancholy. "I wish I could help him be as sure of his calling as I am. He'll be miserable if he tries to do anything else."

Dad nodded again. "The Apostle Paul described it best when he wrote in the book of Romans, 'God's gifts and call are irrevocable.'* Do you see how your assurance is

*Romans 11:29 (NIV)

the balance Dylan needs?"

"I've tried to tell him every way I know how, but it hasn't helped." She shrugged. "I've decided all I can do is keep praying he'll let God convince him."

"He still needs to hear it from you," Dad encouraged. "His love for you makes you the perfect amplifier for his Heavenly Father's voice. I sense he already knows the oil field isn't really an option, but he's afraid to admit it."

Bewilderment pulled her eyebrows together. "Do you know why he's afraid, Dad? I've never before seen him hesitate to commit himself to what he knows is right."

Dad set down his empty mug and reached for Mum's hand, still keeping one arm around her shoulders. "Truly effective ministry makes a person as vulnerable as being in love. Based on how I would have felt in similar circumstances, I think Dylan hid his vulnerability in being over-protective of you. James's gossip made him realize he can't guard you from all unpleasantness, and the board's reaction showed him how deeply he can be hurt. In other words, he's coping with two difficult revelations simultaneously."

What she heard made Leslie long to enfold Dylan in a hug and never let go. She propped her elbows on her knees and her head in her hands, wishing there were some way to ease his turmoil.

As if sensing her feelings, Dad knelt on the floor in front of her and placed his hands around hers, forcing her to look at him. "He knows how much you care, Leslie. Because of the love you share, you have to let him make his own peace with himself. I have no doubt you both will make through just fine."

fourteen

Leslie had finished her homework by the time Dylan arrived Saturday afternoon, freshly fallen snow clinging to his dark hair even after he'd removed his coat. After accepting his kiss, she wrapped her arms around his chest and held him tightly. Slowly, he responded in kind. Their hug lingered for several minutes until he asked, "Any particular reason for this demonstration?"

The laughter in his voice lightened her heart. "I wanted to remind you I'm your friend as well as your sweetheart."

For the first time in over a month, the barriers behind his eyes dropped, letting her see into his heart once more. He swallowed hard a couple of times before answering in a husky whisper. "Hearing you say so means the world to me."

Any words with which she tried to frame her reply sounded trite, even trivial. She hugged him again, hoping her embrace would communicate her faith in him, her admiration for him, and her commitment to a future with him.

The front door opened behind him, and Andrew's voice inquired, "Are you two going to help us, or spend the rest of the afternoon getting in our way with sentimental mush?"

Dylan kept one arm around Leslie as he turned slowly toward the door, his tone heavy with mock indignation. "You'd better have a good reason for interrupting important communication, young man."

Andrew rolled his eyes upward, a large cardboard box

in his arms. "I'd like help getting through the door with this, for starters."

Dylan obediently claimed the box. Andrew picked up another one from the porch floor and handed it in to Leslie. As he picked up a third, Dad appeared on the steps behind him with a fourth.

"Who's moving in?" Dylan asked, following Leslie into the living room.

She winked at him. "Christmas." Setting her box on the floor, she opened it and began removing tinsel, garland, and ribbon.

"What's today's date?" He looked disoriented, like someone awakening in an unfamiliar room.

"December 18th." She linked her arm through his and smiled up into his eyes. "You still have a week to buy my present."

He planted a light kiss on her nose. "I bought it six months ago. I just hadn't noticed Christmas creeping up on us."

"Where've you been, pal?" Andrew shook his head with disdain. "Street decorations have been up for a month."

"Just busy, I guess."

His careless shrug didn't fool Leslie, who felt dejection envelop him again. She pushed aside her own answering heartache to challenge Andrew playfully, "Since you know so much, why don't you set up the tree?"

"Gladly," he chirped, exuberance oozing from every pore. "I'll make this plastic baby look fresh-picked from the woods."

"Joanne," Dad called. "We need your supervision in here."

Mum hurried into the living room with a tray of glasses filled with eggnog. "What for?"

Dad grimaced. "I never know what to do with the

furniture to make room for the tree."

"It's the same every year, honey." Mum laughed. "Move the piano closer to the dining room table, put the couch and the loveseat in an L with the couch along this wall, and push the recliner closer to the loveseat. The tree goes in the corner beside the window." The men quickly followed her instructions. "See?" She grinned impishly at Dad. "Just like a jigsaw puzzle."

Dad clapped Dylan on the shoulder. "Here's a bit of advice for your marriage, Dylan. Let your wife manage the furniture. She makes it look easy, but if you try it on your own, you'll find yourself in a mess."

Dylan's laugh sounded genuine. "I'll keep it in mind. How do I keep out of trouble this afternoon?"

Leslie handed him a string of lights. "How about putting these around the window? These tacks should hold them up."

Three hours and at least a gallon of eggnog later, the house stood fully adorned for the holidays. Leslie heard the front door open and peered around Dylan, where he teetered on a chair affixing a spring of mistletoe to the doorway between the entry and the hall. "Don't take this seriously," Dylan joked in greeting as Vince set his suitcases on the floor and kicked the door shut.

She squeezed around the chair to give her brother a hug. "Welcome home, Vinny."

"It's good to be home." He sounded genuinely pleased.

The next seven days passed quickly in a flurry of baking, shopping, wrapping, and simply enjoying one another's company. Even the animosity between Andrew and Vince had softened, as if in recognition of the season. Leslie found herself savoring individual moments, as though trying to slow time, to wring every last drop of love and family togetherness from each second.

Christmas Eve fell on Friday. With all of her prepara-
tions completed since Monday, she spent most of the day
in the living room, snuggled under a comforter and reading the sequel to the novel she'd finished a month ago. Her
family created a steady stream of traffic in and out as they
placed their last-minute presents beneath the tree.

Sometime after noon, Dad joined her, carrying two cin-
namon buns on napkins. "Mum said we were on our own
for lunch today." He offered her one of the buns. "Would
you like something to drink?"

"Maybe later." She bit into the fluffy sweetness. "Are
you all ready for tonight?"

He grinned smugly. "Absolutely. Is Dylan coming over?"

"He said he'd be here as soon as he wakes up. Last night
was his last shift until Tuesday."

"What time does he usually get home from work?" Glints
of mischief appeared in Dad's eyes.

"Eightish, I think. Why?"

He studied his watch. "I'd figure he's had about six hours
sleep, which should do for today." Grinning with fun, he
walked over to the phone, punched in seven numbers, and
waited. Leslie could tell when Dylan answered because
Dad's grin widened. "Good morning, sleepyhead. . .Oh,
about two in the afternoon. . .I just thought you'd like time
to pack your suitcase before coming over here. . .Didn't
Leslie tell you? Your name is on the guest room door for
the holidays. . .Nonsense, you're part of the family. . .Just
try to be here before it gets dark. She gets owly if we make
her wait too long before opening presents. . .Okay, see you
in an hour or so." He hung up with a look of supreme
satisfaction. "He's awake now."

Leslie giggled. "In that case, I'd better go get ready."

She took her time in the shower, luxuriating in the feeling of not being in a rush. Since red brought out the worst in her skin tone and hair color, she used gold accents to give her favorite forest green a holiday look. A couple of years ago her parents had given her a long, dark green sweater woven with metallic gold highlights. It made the perfect Christmas outfit when combined with matching green stirrup pants and socks. A year ago, she and Dylan had been little more than acquaintances, she realized with a start while blow-drying her hair. Twelve months had brought major changes to her world. She left her hair loose, the way Dylan liked it best, and put on a pair of gold dangly earrings. Just a few moments in front of her makeup mirror left her satisfied with her appearance.

When she returned downstairs, Dad passed in the hallway, carrying the coffee table to the family room. In the living room she noticed he'd put beanbags from the family room in its place and plugged in the lights on the tree. Vince sprawled on the couch, looking unusually content. "You look festive, little sister," he greeted her.

"Thank you." She settled into one of the bean bags and turned so she could face both him and the Christmas tree. "You look happy to be home."

A commotion in the entry that could only be Brad Ferguson dispelled the serenity. Something heavy landed on the floor with a thump, and Li'l Brad squealed, "Gamma!" Leslie felt a poignant rush of delight, listening to the mingle of voices—Mum and Karen exchanging sentimental holiday greetings, a short comment from Dad, and Big Brad's boisterous laugh.

"Somehow the house seems smaller when he arrives," Vince commented quietly, though his smile removed any possible criticism from his words.

"Ho, ho, ho!" The man under discussion stepped over Leslie and poured the contents of a box on the floor beside the tree.

"Brad!" Karen exclaimed in distress. "You'll wreck the bows."

"Nah. They're fine. See?" He held a wrinkled specimen up as demonstration.

The rest of the family laughed at the familiar annual routine. Dad observed, "We wouldn't recognize presents from the Fergusons if they weren't mangled."

Then, through the babble of simultaneous conversations, Leslie heard the front door open again. In a moment, she'd scrambled to her feet and dashed to the entry. Seeing Dylan there, his arms full of colorful parcels, made her feel like Christmas had finally and completely arrived. His marvelous green eyes brightened with admiration. "You look so good, we don't need any other decorations. Would you do something with these?" He leaned over to transfer the presents from his arms to his and dropped a quick kiss on her lips at the same time.

"Merry Christmas to you, too." She turned to take her load into the living room, but his whisper stopped her.

"Do something with those, then come back here, please."

She didn't need to be invited twice. No one in the other room seemed to notice her entrance with the presents or her speedy exit. When she returned to the entry, Dylan had removed his coat and boots and stood waiting with the incredible smile meant just for her. He'd chosen to wear black jeans and the sweater she liked best, a bulky knit garment that matched the color of her outfit and emphasized the vivid green of his eyes. "We match," she observed playfully.

He enfolded her in an intense hug. "In hearts as well as

in clothes," he whispered into her hair. Keeping his arms around her, he pulled back to look into her face. "I just wanted to have you all to myself for a couple of moments before we join the crowd."

"Shall we go in now, or wait until they come looking for us?"

He winked. "Let's surprise them."

Andrew followed them in, and Mum came right behind with glasses of eggnog. As if on cue, conversation abated and everyone else settled into comfortable positions around the room. Vince occupied the recliner, Karen pulled Li'l Brad up to sit snugly between her and Big Brad on the loveseat, Dad, Mum and Andrew filled the couch, and Dylan and Leslie relaxed on their beanbags.

"We must be ready to begin." Dad looked around the room with joy in his eyes. "If nothing else this year, we've learned we can't count on anything staying the same. Every time our entire family is together is a bonus which I've learned to treasure. Of course, we have one more family member with us this year than we had last year. Welcome to the crowd, Dylan."

Leslie felt Dylan's arm drape across her shoulders, so she snuggled back against him while Dad continued. "Your joining the family may mean Leslie won't be with us at this time next year, but this seems as good a time as any to make sure you know we're all delighted you two found each other." The rest of the family applauded, and Big Brad let loose a piercing whistle. Dad grinned. "We'd also like to express appreciation for your quieter personality as compared to other individuals we won't name." Karen gave her husband a look of pure admiration and Vince laughed aloud. Dad enfolded Mum's hand in his. "Joanne and I thank our Heavenly Father every day for each one of you

He's put in our family, and we want to let you know how much we love and appreciate you. Now, before Li'l Brad starts getting fidgety, let's read the Christmas story." He opened his Bible and began with the familiar words. "And it came to pass in those days that there went out a decree from Caesar Augustus. . . ."*

Leslie loved to hear his deep voice rise and fall with the cadence of the old English found in the King James version of the Bible. Though the family had long used other translations, he always read the Christmas story in the older version. Even Li'l Brad seemed captured by the thoughtful hush invoked by the story. He sucked his thumb and remained curled up against his dad without restraint. She turned her head to look at Dylan. Tears stood in his eyes and his arm tightened around her. A new peace glowed softly behind the tears.

All too soon, Dad reached the end of the passage. ". . . and the shepherds returned, glorifying and praising God for all the things that they had heard and seen, as it was told unto them."** He closed the Bible and looked around the room slowly with affection. "If Christmas ended right here, it would be enough for me."

"Amen," Brad boomed solemnly, and a wave of laughter lifted the solemnity. Li'l Brad sat up and looked at his mother with shining eyes. "Pwesents?"

"Yes," she told him. "Do you want to help hand them out?"

With a definitive nod, he bounded off his dad's lap and headed straight for the tree. Karen quickly joined him before he could help himself. Picking up the nearest package, she read the label, then handed the parcel to her son.

*Luke 2:1 KJV
**Luke 2:20

"Can you give this to Grandpa?"

His little face beamed at being allowed to help with something so important. He clutched the present tightly and toddled over to Dad, who accepted it with a solemn, "Thank you, Brad."

Though Leslie had heard of families who opened their presents all at once, she preferred her family's custom. Each person took a turn opening one present at a time. Everyone had a chance to appreciate all the gifts, and the process prolonged the joy of the evening. She'd received a new pair of ice skates from Vince and an elegant tan coat dress from Karen and Brad when Li'l Brad brought her a small package labeled "To Leslie, with love, Dylan." She removed each piece of tape carefully and folded back the wrapping. The larger cardboard box concealed a velvet-covered jeweler's case. Inside the case lay a bracelet made of interlocking heart outlines. Two hearts in the center were solid. One had been engraved with Leslie's initials, LJC, and the other with Dylan's, DJS. She lifted it from the case tenderly. "Dylan, it's lovely. Would you put it on for me?" His fingers fumbled with the clasp, but he eventually managed to fasten it around her wrist. Attention moved on to Andrew. Leslie continued studying her gift, examining the engraved letters, turning the bracelet on her arm to watch it reflect the colored lights from the tree.

"I'm glad you like it," Dylan whispered, leaning close.

Brad didn't miss the opportunity to tease. "Hey! No necking over there!"

"Mind your own business," Dylan shot back, his smile telling Leslie they'd continue the discussion later.

At long last, Karen uncovered the package that contained Leslie's present to Dylan. Her son reached for it eagerly. "It's for Uncle Dylan," she explained, "but I think it's a little heavy for you to carry. May I help?"

"No. Me do." He tried to take the box from her, but as soon as she let go, it slipped from his grasp. "Little bit help," he decided, amid indulgent chuckles.

Dylan accepted the package with a hug for the small delivery person. "Would you like to help me unwrap it?"

Li'l Brad's eyes lit with eagerness, but he looked at his mother for reassurance. "Go ahead. Uncle Dylan said you can."

With a chortle of glee, he attacked the wrapping with both hands, quickly reducing it to shreds. He tried to reach into the box when Dylan opened it, but Leslie pulled him into her lap. "Let Uncle Dylan do this part himself." She watched Dylan's eyes as he lifted out one hardbound volume after another.

"This has to be everything Phillip Keller has ever written!" His admiring tone left no doubt as to his appreciation of the gift. "You must have had quite a challenge finding them all!"

"A bit," she conceded, "but I've been told I'm a determined person."

Vince guffawed. "If that isn't the understatement of the season!"

She fixed him with a look of disdain. "Some people appreciate my talents."

Eventually the last present was opened and admired. Li'l Brad danced around in the discarded wrapping paper, more interested in increasing the mess than examining the gifts he'd received. Leslie and Mum set an array of snack food on the table, along with coffee, tea and more eggnog. Leslie marveled again at the change Christmas had wrought in the loved ones who'd worried her the most. Vince's arrogant distance had vanished. Andrew's frightened sullenness had disappeared. Most importantly, Dylan's eyes remained bright and clear with the joy of the season. She made a point of hugging each family member as they came by for munchies.

When Brad and Karen left for home a couple of hours later, she felt as though an idyllic interlude slipped away. Andrew went to bed, and Vince vanished into his room. Leslie and Dylan stuffed empty boxes and torn wrapping paper into garbage bags while Dad and Mum put food away. Though the four reconvened in the living room later, the base of the tree looked as barren as the empty recliner and love seat.

Leslie awoke early Christmas morning. Though her bed-side clock read twenty minutes after six, she didn't feel the need for any more sleep. Wrapping her mint green and peach flower housecoat around herself, she tiptoed down to the Christmas tree and plugged in the lights. The glowing colors cast just enough light in the room to make it feel cozy. She curled her legs under her at one end of the loveseat and gazed dreamily at the shimmering spectacle. This time next year, she'd be in her own living room in her and Dylan's home, enjoying a tree they'd decorated together. Something deeper than intuition assured her he'd still be pastoring.

The other half of her dreams wandered into the room, one of Mum's quilts draped around his shoulders. "You're up early," he whispered.

She moved her feet so he could sit close beside her. "I didn't feel like sleeping any more."

He wrapped the blanket around them both, drawing her into his arms. "I know what you mean. This time of year makes a person reluctant to miss a single, special moment."

"Are you planning to spend any of your days off with

your parents?"

"Not this week." He hugged her tighter. "I have Friday and Monday off for New Year's and Pastor Jim doesn't mind if I'm gone for the weekend. Would you like to come home with me?"

"I'd love to."

A precious silence fell over them, enhancing the joy of simply being together. It could have been a few minutes or an hour later when Dylan finally spoke again. "The Christmas story spoke something new to me last night."

Leslie moved around to drape her legs across his lap so she could stay close to him yet still see his eyes. "What was it?"

"Even though God gave Mary the job of giving birth to Jesus, He also gave Joseph a responsibility. I finally understand that when He brings two people together with love, His calling on one includes both. I've been wrestling with His calling for me as a pastor partly because I felt the calling would be unfair to you. I realized last night He's called us both, which means He'll give you whatever you need to cope with the challenges of being a pastor's wife. My desire to shield you from the ministry was actually denying you the joy of being my partner. Much of the strength I've needed in the last couple of months, He tried to give through you. You are part of the strength He's given me to accompany His calling."

The note of awe in his voice brought tears to her eyes. "You're now sure of what you're supposed to do?"

Deep love glowed in his eyes. "I know I won't be happy if I run away from Heritage. I still loathe the way people like Henry Dunn can turn what's supposed to be ministry into politics, but I guess it's something I'll just have to learn to cope with."

In an outburst of impulsive joy, she gave him a neck-strangling hug. "You've just given me the best of all Christmas presents. Welcome back, Pastor Stoddard."

fifteen

Less than a week later, Dylan and Leslie set out for Bayfield. The six hours of travel time passed quickly. Dylan's newfound peace made Leslie feel as though her best friend had returned from a long absence. Once again, laughter and fun punctuated their togetherness, along with discussions of a more serious nature.

"Has Andrew said anything to you lately about me?" Dylan asked at one point.

"He hasn't been talking much about anything."

He reached over and squeezed her hand. "He's doing better than you might think, Les'. He told me about the letter from Dr. Wallace and your dad's ultimatum. I think he's finally realized he has a problem which won't simply go away if he ignores it long enough. How would you feel if I signed the counseling agreement with him?"

"Andrew actually asked you to work with him? I think it's terrific!"

Dylan smiled at her enthusiasm. "I was pretty flabbergasted myself when he mentioned it. He went with me to talk to Pastor Jim about it, since I wondered if I'm too close to your family to do any good. However, Pastor Jim feels Andrew already trusts me, which he says is the first hurdle in any counseling relationship. I told Andrew I'd have to talk with you about it before I could commit."

"I'm impressed he's even attempting to cooperate with Dad. If you're the one he respects enough to talk with, who am I to object?"

"He wants to go to Bible school more than anyone realizes. He hasn't told me why yet, but he seems to feel it's important for whatever his future goals are."

"Wow." Leslie could hardly believe what she heard.

"I know what you mean." Dylan grinned. "I still feel much the same way. It just proves you can never second guess what's happening in another person's mind."

It felt sublime to be talking things over with him again. "I love Andrew too much to ever give up on him, but there have been days when he's stretched my hoping capacity to the limit. Our last family council was one of those times. He left so upset, I wouldn't have been surprised if he'd dropped out of school and run away from home."

"I don't think the thought ever entered his mind." He spoke with confidence. "For one thing, he'd never do anything deliberately to hurt you. Like I mentioned before, he also has a personal goal of some kind for what he wants to do with his life. I wouldn't be surprised if that sense of purpose is what's kept him away from the bottle since his accident."

"He's been irate with anyone who's mentioned the possibility of him drinking again. He reacted almost like he had a guilty conscience."

"Or perhaps talking about it made him feel even more vulnerable to the temptation."

"I'm just glad he's willing to talk with you about it."

The three days with the Stoddards were filled with the same feeling of family Leslie had experienced at her own home the week before. She easily referred to Dylan's parents as Mom and Dad, just as he did. Their smiles told her how much she'd pleased them. Sunday morning at church, she met the pastor he'd told her so much about. Pastor Terry's sermon reminded her of the conversational, easy way in which Dylan taught scriptural lessons. In the evening, while Steve went somewhere else with friends, Dylan told his parents about what he'd experienced since September. He sat on the couch with his arm around Leslie's shoulders, and his parents faced them from a pair of easy chairs on the other side of the coffee table. When he mentioned his frustration with the deacons, Dad Stoddard's eyes twinkled. "I get the feeling you haven't been reading much in the Gospels lately, son."

Dylan looked startled. "Why do you say that?"

"Jesus spent the entire three years of His ministry on earth continuously struggling with people like the men you describe. Anyone who wants to follow Him wholeheartedly is bound to experience the same."

"Hmmm." Dylan mused. "Somehow I hadn't thought about my experiences in light of Jesus' ministry before."

"Because of the way his earthly ministry ended, we like to think of what Jesus accomplished as being so divine it has no relevance to our lives beyond salvation." Dad Stoddard's expression reminded Leslie of Dylan's during some of the best Sunday school lessons. "What I read in the Gospels, though, makes me think He spent those three and a half years wandering through Judea and Galilee to show us what to expect when we endeavor to communicate His love and to give us an example for how to respond."

Dylan gave a little laugh. "It's so obvious when you point it out, but somehow I never looked at the Gospel story quite that way before. It looks like I'll have to do some serious reading."

"Not too serious," his mother cautioned with a grin. "God created laughter, too."

Dylan pulled on the back of Leslie's hair. "This lady

does a good job of making sure I don't take myself too seriously."

"She's as good a balance for you as your mother's been for me." Dad Stoddard included both women in his look of pride.

The discussion drifted into other topics. "Have you heard from Ron and Jenine lately?" Dylan asked.

Leslie recognized the sorrow in Mom Stoddard's eyes at the reference to her only daughter. "About a month ago, Ron called to let us know he'd had to put her in the hospital again. We asked if we could come visit, but he said she didn't even want him around. He called again last week to say she'd finally gained enough weight to be released, and said he'd let us know when she seemed to have recovered enough to cope with visitors."

"We couldn't have chosen a better husband for Jenine if we'd picked him ourselves," Dad Stoddard observed. Then his eyes twinkled again and he looked at Leslie. "I think our future daughter-in-law is of the same quality."

The ring of the telephone saved Leslie from having to answer. Mom answered, then beckoned to Dylan. "It's your pastor."

With a sinking feeling, Leslie watched Dylan pick up the receiver. "Hello?. . .Yes?. . ." A look of incredible delight spread from his eyes to cover his entire face. "Would you mind repeating that, Pastor Jim?. . .Who am I to turn down a miracle?. . .Thanks for calling." He set the receiver down gently. Three strides brought him to the couch, where he pulled Leslie up to whirl her around in an ecstatic hug. "You'll never believe it! You'll never believe it!" he kept saying.

She finally forced him to stand still and release her. "What won't I believe?"

He looked at her, laughed aloud, then looked at his parents and laughed again. Finally, he took a deep breath, and tried to speak. "Henry Dunn. . . ." Jubilant laughter broke from him again.

"Dylan," Leslie threatened, grabbing his arms and shaking him gently. "If you don't tell me what's going on, I'm calling Pastor Jim."

"Okay." He took another deep breath. "After church this morning, Henry Dunn called the board together and announced he thinks Heritage needs me full time." Stopping to swallow another burst of laughter, he continued unsteadily. "Since no one disagreed, they authorized Pastor Jim to offer me two thousand dollars a month, with an increase to three thousand when we get married." He whirled Leslie again.

Tears of joy ran down Mom's face. "Isn't that wonderful?"

Dad Stoddard simply beamed with delight. He waited until Dylan had calmed a bit, then suggested, "I think there's Someone we need to thank."

With an expression of utter humility, Dylan took Leslie's hand in his and knelt beside the couch. Mom and Dad moved to kneel with them.

"My Father," Dylan's voice broke, but he cleared his throat and continued. "Thank you seems totally inadequate after all You've done to bring me to the fulfillment of the dream You gave me so many years ago. Not only have You given me a wonderful place in which to minister and a mentor who walks with You as I want to do, but You've also provided me with a special partner with whom I can share the joys and struggles of Your calling." His voice broke again, and Leslie felt tears dripping on their joined hands. When he couldn't continue, Dad Stoddard picked up the prayer. "Bless these two, our Lord, as they follow You with all their hearts. May they never forget the wonder of this moment, and never doubt their calling is of You. In the name of Jesus, who's walked this way before us, Amen."

A Letter To Our Readers

Dear Reader:

In order that we might better contribute to your reading enjoyment, we would appreciate your taking a few minutes to respond to the following questions. When completed, please return to the following:

Rebecca Germany, Editor
Heartsong Presents
P.O. Box 719
Uhrichsville, Ohio 44683

1. Did you enjoy reading *Dancing in the Darkness*?
   ❑ Very much. I would like to see more books
      by this author!
   ❑ Moderately
      I would have enjoyed it more if _____

   _____

2. Are you a member of **Heartsong Presents**? ❑Yes ❑No
   If no, where did you purchase this book?_____

   _____

3. What influenced your decision to purchase this
   book? (Check those that apply.)

   ❑ Cover   ❑ Back cover copy

   ❑ Title   ❑ Friends

   ❑ Publicity   ❑ Other_____

4. How would you rate, on a scale from 1 (poor) to 5
   (superior), **Heartsong Presents'** new cover design?_____

5. On a scale from 1 (poor) to 10 (superior), please rate the following elements.

___Heroine   ___Plot

___Hero   ___Inspirational theme

___Setting   ___Secondary characters

6. What settings would you like to see covered in **Heartsong Presents** books?_____

_____

_____

7. What are some inspirational themes you would like to see treated in future books?_____

_____

_____

8. Would you be interested in reading other **Heartsong Presents** titles?   ❏ Yes   ❏ No

9. Please check your age range:
   ❏ Under 18   ❏ 18-24   ❏ 25-34
   ❏ 35-45   ❏ 46-55   ❏ Over 55

10. How many hours per week do you read? _____

Name _____

Occupation_____

Address_____

City_____ State_____ Zip_____

Stories of Peace

by Janelle Burnham

___River of Peace___—The remote village of Dawson Creek, British Columbia, has never had a schoolteacher before Ida Thomas. Of all her students Ida finds herself drawn to Ruth McEvan, who like Ida is struggling with a devastating family tragedy. While scorning the attentions of one man, will Ida find a man she can truly love, a man to fill her empty heart? HP100

___Beckoning Streams___—Should Ruth McEvan remain in the familiar Peace River region and raise a family with the kind-hearted and marriage-minded Jed Spencer? The tragedy that claimed Ruth's mother and three brothers years earlier has hardened her heart. Why risk love when it can be taken away? HP119

___Winding Highway___—No longer the elegant pastor's wife of Winnipeg, Jerusha is now taking in laundry to support herself and her brother. Yet the warmth of the townspeople in Dawson Creek and the attentions of one special army man bring Jerusha a unique sense of joy. When the war beckons, however, Jerusha must face the winding highway of life alone, perhaps forever. HP139

·····Heart♥ng····

Any 12 *Heartsong Presents* titles for only $26.95 **

CONTEMPORARY ROMANCE IS CHEAPER BY THE DOZEN!

Buy any assortment of twelve *Heartsong Presents* titles and save 25% off the already discounted price of $2.95 each!

**plus $1.00 shipping and handling per order and sales tax where applicable.

HEARTSONG PRESENTS TITLES AVAILABLE NOW:

_HP 3 RESTORE THE JOY, *Sara Mitchell*
_HP 4 REFLECTIONS OF THE HEART, *Sally Laity**
_HP 5 THIS TREMBLING CUP, *Marlene Chase*
_HP 6 THE OTHER SIDE OF SILENCE, *Marlene Chase*
_HP 9 HEARTSTRINGS, *Irene B. Brand**
_HP 10 SONG OF LAUGHTER, *Lauraine Snelling**
_HP 13 PASSAGE OF THE HEART, *Kjersti Hoff Baez*
_HP 14 A MATTER OF CHOICE, *Susannah Hayden*
_HP 18 LLAMA LADY, *VeraLee Wiggins**
_HP 19 ESCORT HOMEWARD, *Eileen M. Berger**
_HP 21 GENTLE PERSUASION, *Veda Boyd Jones*
_HP 22 INDY GIRL, *Brenda Bancroft*
_HP 25 REBAR, *Mary Carpenter Reid*
_HP 26 MOUNTAIN HOUSE, *Mary Louise Colln*
_HP 29 FROM THE HEART, *Sara Mitchell*
_HP 30 A LOVE MEANT TO BE, *Brenda Bancroft*
_HP 33 SWEET SHELTER, *VeraLee Wiggins*
_HP 34 UNDER A TEXAS SKY, *Veda Boyd Jones*
_HP 37 DRUMS OF SHELOMOH, *Yvonne Lehman*
_HP 38 A PLACE TO CALL HOME, *Eileen M. Berger*
_HP 41 FIELDS OF SWEET CONTENT, *Norma Jean Lutz*
_HP 42 SEARCH FOR TOMORROW, *Mary Hawkins*
_HP 45 DESIGN FOR LOVE, *Janet Gortsema*
_HP 46 THE GOVERNOR'S DAUGHTER, *Veda Boyd Jones*
_HP 49 YESTERDAY'S TOMORROWS, *Linda Herring*
_HP 50 DANCE IN THE DISTANCE, *Kjersti Hoff Baez*
_HP 53 MIDNIGHT MUSIC, *Janelle Burnham*
_HP 54 HOME TO HER HEART, *Lena Nelson Dooley*
_HP 57 LOVE'S SILKEN MELODY, *Norma Jean Lutz*
_HP 58 FREE TO LOVE, *Doris English*
_HP 61 PICTURE PERFECT, *Susan Kirby*
_HP 62 A REAL AND PRECIOUS THING, *Brenda Bancroft*
_HP 65 ANGEL FACE, *Frances Carfi Matranga*
_HP 66 AUTUMN LOVE, *Ann Bell*
_HP 69 BETWEEN LOVE AND LOYALTY, *Susannah Hayden*
_HP 70 A NEW SONG, *Kathleen Yapp*
_HP 73 MIDSUMMER'S DREAM, *Rena Eastman*
_HP 74 SANTANONI SUNRISE, *Hope Irvin Marston and Claire M. Coughlin*
_HP 77 THE ROAD BEFORE ME, *Susannah Hayden**
_HP 78 A SIGN OF LOVE, *Veda Boyd Jones**
_HP 81 BETTER THAN FRIENDS, *Sally Laity*

*Temporarily out of stock.

(If ordering from this page, please remember to include it with the order form.)

Presents

*Temporarily out of stock.

Great Inspirational Romance at a Great Price!

Heartsong Presents books are inspirational romances in contemporary and historical settings, designed to give you an enjoyable, spirit-lifting reading experience. You can choose from 148 wonderfully written titles from some of today's best authors like Colleen L. Reece, Brenda Bancroft, Janelle Jamison, and many others.

When ordering quantities less than twelve, above titles are $2.95 each.

Heartsong Presents
Love Stories Are Rated G!

That's for godly, gratifying, and of course, great! If you love a thrilling love story, but don't appreciate the sordidness of some popular paperback romances, **Heartsong Presents** is for you. In fact, **Heartsong Presents** is the *only inspirational romance book club*, the only one featuring love stories where Christian faith is the primary ingredient in a marriage relationship.

Sign up today to receive your first set of four, never before published Christian romances. Send no money now; you will receive a bill with the first shipment. You may cancel at any time without obligation, and if you aren't completely satisfied with any selection, you may return the books for an immediate refund!

Imagine. . .four new romances every four weeks—two historical, two contemporary—with men and women like you who long to meet the one God has chosen as the love of their lives. . .all for the low price of $9.97 postpaid.

To join, simply complete the coupon below and mail to the address provided. **Heartsong Presents** romances are rated G for another reason: They'll arrive *Godspeed!*